SIERA LONDON

I0667106

GOING THE DISTANCE

The Men of Endurance

GOING THE DISTANCE
The Men of Endurance

Copyright © 2018 K. PRINGLE

Print ISBN-13: 978-1-949263-00-8

http://www.sieralondon.com[1]

Cover art by Fantasia Frog Designs

Edited by Gayla Leath, Dark Dreams Editing

First Edition, July 2018

All rights reserved.

DEDICATION

Thank you to my friend and fellow author Olivia Gaines for dreaming up this serial romance about single fathers. Olivia gave me free rein to create this beautiful town called Endurance and fill it with all the charm of small town life and rich friendships. The town of Endurance is based on the city of Auburn, California, the endurance sports capital of the United States. Throughout each book in the Men of Endurance series, you'll discover fun facts about Auburn and the rich history of Placer County. If you're new to this story world, be sure to read *A Walk Through Endurance*, where Abel Burney and Julie Kratzner will introduce you to this town called Endurance.

To all my faithful readers, thank you from the bottom of my heart for sharing Siera London Books. You make this journey worthwhile. This love story is dedicated to Simone Choi, of Black Women Swirl Literature, LaSheera Lee of Read You Later, and Mrs. Toni Bonita. Each of you spread joy at every opportunity and I appreciate your acts of service and dedication to our booklover community.

Blessings Romancelandia, Siera

Let us run with endurance the race that is set before us.

Hebrews 12:1

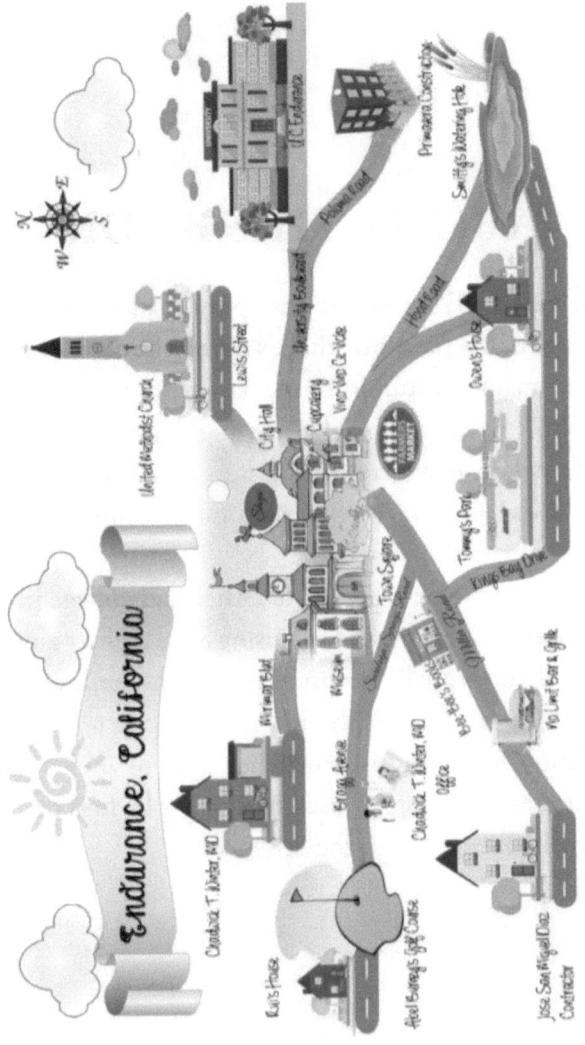

Endurance, California

ABOUT THIS BOOK

The "risk it all" student. The "play it safe" professor. An improbable pair, but there's no textbook for love.

Music major Autumn Raine is used to taking care of herself. So, when an eight-year-old's prank brings her face-to-face with her secret crush, she's grateful for the rescue but this close encounter has Autumn wishing for private lessons.

After a failed marriage, single father and college professor Rui Conners was committed to raising his daughter alone. But, Autumn is bandaging his wounded heart one smile at a time.

What's the problem? She has no idea he's interested and Rui's relationship with his ex-wife is far from ancient history. How will these two people, used to flying solo, find the perfect note to make their duet go the distance?

CHAPTER ONE

F or Autumn Raine, early mornings in Endurance were the perfect time to think and put ten extra miles on the pavement. With sweat dripping down her face, she turned onto University Boulevard, giving her muscles free rein. Breathing in, she pulled the cool September mountain air deep into her lungs, using the adrenaline high to pump her arms and push the Reebok Floatrides hugging her feet harder. Now she needed her brain to use the added oxygen to conjure up a solution for earning the last five hundred dollars of her rent payment. She had nothing left to sell.

Eight months ago, at the age of twenty-six, she'd packed up her hopes, fears, and dreams to relocate from San Diego to this northern California town, in the sprawling foothills of the Sierra Nevada. Though not as temperate as the southern border of the state, the rugged peaks, majestic grape vineyards, and four-seasons Mediterranean climate held a certain magic for Autumn. Home to the University of California, Endurance, this was her second chance at the future she'd written about in all those girly journals tucked away in her hope chest. Here in Endurance, where city hall held the town's only post office and the public library shared the same space as the art museum, life was beautifully simple. If she could figure out how to keep food on the table, a roof over her head, the car running, and finish her bachelor's degree, then life would be simply perfect.

That's where the daily runs entered the equation. Each year, more than 900,000 extreme sports enthusiasts flocked to the State Recreational Park to participate in the man vs. nature races of all kinds. Six months of sweat, pain, and determination, but Autumn's sacrifice would be worth the journey in the end. In three weeks, she'd face the ultimate challenge, a one-hundred-mile foot race through the California hill country. The prize-seventy-five thousand dollars towards a college degree with her name embossed in gold script. In some ways, Autumn was in the race of her life. She had a future to secure.

Autumn's first attempt at completing her four-year degree had been derailed by her cult-like worship of a man. According to her aunt, love was a coin toss. A few women got a head start with a good guy, but most ended up with an unlimited supply of tails. Autumn didn't put much credence in anything her aunt believed, but love sat low on her list of priorities. Though a certain professor had caught her eye and she still envisioned a future husband and a few kids, Autumn heeded the voice of experience and trampled the longing under foot.

Ignoring the burn in her glutes and gut, she tuned in to the music flowing through her earbuds. Music had a relaxing effect, so she let the soulful voice of Aria Arie loosen her muscles, fill her thoughts, and fuel her body to move. In her mind, she saw her stride lengthening and the cells firing in every part of her body. Power hummed through her limbs. She was in her zone. This was her year to succeed where she'd failed in the past.

As she approached town, people started to appear on the street. Julie, the Sport Complicated reporter, attempted to pedal her bike up the hill on Miller Road, probably leaving the Farmers Market. With her sunny smile and inquisitive eyes, the full-figured beauty had made progress in her physical fitness.

"Hi, Julie," Autumn said, with a wave of her hand. It wasn't so long ago, Doctor Chadwick Winter, the only pediatrician for miles, had found the woman sprawled on her front porch after a short walk to Ma Hildie's Grocers.

"Looking good," Julie called back, her breath a little short. "One day that will be me."

Lifting her hand, Autumn gave a thumbs up gesture in support. Picking up speed, she scanned the area for Abel Burney. Abel owned the local golf course on the outskirts of town and she suspected Julie owned his heart.

Rounding the corner onto Hood Lane, Autumn crossed the parking lot surrounding Tommy's Park and then stumbled to a halt. She tried to process the scene unfolding before her. A girl, somewhere between eight or ten, sat behind the wheel of a 2001 VW Beetle, Autumn's not so gently used dark blue beetle. The little cutie, with twin braids hanging down her back and brown eyes narrowed in concentration, was turning the key. In a small town like Endurance it was pretty common to find back doors unlocked and car keys tucked in the sun visor. The grind of the ignition was a stark contrast to the quiet of morning. When the engine caught, the soft hum of the motor spurred Autumn into action. She shot forward, quickly yanking the car door open. Dressed in a red and blue striped shirt, blue jeans, and sneakers, she looked like a girl scout. With a sure, but gentle grip Autumn dropped a hand on the kid's shoulder. The would-be car jacker startled.

"Hey," she yelled, cringing away from Autumn. "What are you doing?"

The nerve of this kid. Keeping a hand in place, Autumn slid her hand over the steering wheel, turned the key, and disengaged the ignition. The clattering engine dropped back into slumber. Where was this girl's parents? Either way, she needed to assume control of the situation.

Autumn shook the girl's shoulder. "Where's your mom?"

"In Europe," she said, snatching her arm away. "Where's yours?"

Autumn's entire nervous system lit up at the insolent tone. Breathe out she told herself. This little girl needed some serious supervision and a major timeout.

Using as stern a voice as she could muster, Autumn said, "Get out of the car. Now."

The little hellion pursed her lips, then rolled her little head on an even smaller neck.

Oh no she didn't.

Hitting Autumn with a narrow-eyed gaze, she asked, "Are you even an adult?"

Mouth open, Autumn couldn't believe the audacity of this kid. "Of course, I'm an adult," she stammered.

The kid gave her a smirk. "You look kind of little to me."

At five feet two, Autumn accepted her petite frame may appear juvenile, but her curves did not.

Sputtering, Autumn felt inclined to defend herself. "Well, I'm not."

Not the best come back, but she wasn't used to verbal sparring with a pre-pubescent child.

"How do I know you're not trying to take the car for yourself?" she charged.

What in the sugar plum fairy? Why would she have to steal her own car? Autumn was about to lose her religion. Considering the closest Baptist church congregation gathered twenty-five miles north of Endurance, in Pine Valley, it might take her a year or two to find it again. The distance suited Autumn just fine. She and God had an understanding. He stayed out of her way, and she returned the favor in kind.

"Who are your parents, young lady?" Autumn insisted, adding a touch more authority to her voice in hopes that the child would come clean. Not that she would call the cops, but still the girl needed a stern talking to.

"Noneya?"

Autumn couldn't recall an Endurance resident named Noneya, but she wasn't good with names or faces.

"Noneya who? What's your last name?"

"Business," she supplied, brown eyes sparkling in defiance.

Autumn lifted her hand, finger leveled at the school-aged comedian. The sheer fact that she was an adult should have motivated the child to cower. Autumn leveled a cautionary gaze on the kid.

"Maybe a visit to the sheriff will locate Mrs. Noneya Business."

Long, dark brown lashes dipped low before a furrow formed between her brows. Good. Time to end this charade. Autumn needed to drive back to her studio apartment, get cleaned up, and then get to the university before her music history class.

"Wait. My dad is in the park. He asked me to warm up the engine. Yeah...yeah, that's it."

Autumn could tell the girl was warming to her lie. "He's teaching me to drive because he's in a wheelchair. He lost his leg when a coyote attacked him on one of the valley trails."

Could this be the truth? Not the car part, but about her father. Visitors and locals injured themselves hiking or running on the original 1850's mining trails from California gold rush days.

"But, you're too young to drive."

With a roll of her eyes, the kid dismissed Autumn's comment like she had time and wisdom on her side.

"I'm eight," she said, her tone communicating her disappointment that Autumn failed to recognize maturity when it graced her presence. "And, my father needs help," she sniffled.

Call it women's intuition, but a ring of truth lay hidden in this child's epic fantasy. For a split second, Autumn wondered if the father truly needed help. Quickly, she glanced over her shoulder, peering through the large oaks guarding the park. Several people, some dressed in bright-colored zippered windbreakers, walked in groups along the dirt track surrounding the park. What she didn't see was a post-coyote bite, wheelchair-bound extreme athlete pushing himself around the happy trail. She chastised herself, of course, this was make-believe.

Not wanting to entertain this tale any longer, Autumn replied, "Your dad sounds like he's in terrible shape. A lot of pain."

The miscreant had the audacity to bat her lashes in hopes of drawing sympathy. "Yeah, it's been hard on me."

"When did it happen?"

The double blink came in sets of three. Autumn had to give the kid her props. She was creative. How long would it take the little thespian to spin the second act?

"When?" she croaked.

Ignoring the guilt that swamped her at egging the child on, Autumn fought to keep a smile from gracing her face.

"Yes. I mean an injury like that takes a long time to heal."

"Huh...yeah. He's been home all week."

Not bad for an eight-year-old's imagination.

Autumn gestured for the kid to get out of the car.

"Come on."

There was no movement from the vehicle. Man, this kid was ballsy. When she was this age, she jumped if she thought her aunt wanted her to do something.

"My mom and dad said to be afraid of strangers."

Autumn's patience, worn thin, crumbled.

"Get out of my car. Right now, young lady."

Enough already. This kid needed a disciplined, but gentle hand, maybe.

All of a sudden, a scream rent the air.

"Stranger danger, stranger danger," the child belted out.

Autumn spun around, looking behind her to assess the threat. Joggers stopped to stare at her and the horror movie scream queen in the car. "No, I don't want to go with you. Please, lady. Leave me alone."

Autumn glared down at her accuser. "What in the sugar plum fairy?"

"Hey," someone called from behind Autumn.

Between the cacophony of raised voices and condemning stares, she was more than aware of their growing audience.

"Get away from that kid," came another voice from a different direction.

Autumn heard someone say they were calling the cops. Oh my goodness, she should have slept-in this morning. This kid was starring in her own off-Broadway drama, and Autumn was the villain.

Autumn threw up her hands. People walking on both sides of the trail paused to watch the unfolding drama.

Sure enough, the sheriff's cruiser appeared in the lot. The door swung wide and out stepped Keith Fullerton. The town sheriff was a regular at No Limit Bar and Grille, where Autumn used to babysit the owner's five-year-old son, Cai. Her arrangement with Owen Tate tapered off after Ivy Summers arrived in town. The two had married in a late July ceremony behind the bar. Owen had spent the better part of the summer constructing a new patio, complete with tiny lights strung from open latticework and pillars wrapped in ivy especially for his bride-to-be. These days, the patio served as outdoor dining with a view of giant Valley Oaks and fir trees leading up the hillside. A third of Endurance's thirteen hundred and thirty-four residents had attended. Cai had counted. Of course, Autumn celebrated their happy ending, but boy had her bank account missed the steady paycheck.

Shooting a glance at the kid, her eyes stretched wide when seeing her looking as relaxed as prima donna in a tiara. Seriously, who was this kid?

Autumn, on the opposite end of the spectrum wiped her sweaty hands on her leggings. She anxiously awaited the sheriff, so he could get to the bottom of this and she could be on her way. Whoever the parents were, they needed to be put under the jail. This kid should be in school. Keith approached, his expression more curious than menacing.

"Hi, Autumn." The sheriff's light brown eyes crinkled at the corners when he looked past her and spied the would-be car thief behind the wheel. He grimaced.

"Simone, shouldn't you be in school?" Keith asked.

Autumn looked from the sheriff to the kid.

"You know her?" Autumn said, surprised the man knew the kid's name.

Keith released a long-suffering sigh. "Yep," he said, tilting his tan cowboy hat with a leather braid back on his head. "I have a long history with Simone and her antics."

The squeak of the door closing drew Autumn's attention. Simone, that's what the sheriff had called her, stood in front of the closed door. The kid offered the sheriff a sickly-sweet smile.

"Good morning, Mr. Policeman. I'll just be heading off to school now."

Autumn watched to see if the sheriff would take the bait or keep her on the hook. His face looked down right pained. What was going on between these two?

"I told you the next time I caught you, your dad and me would have a long talk."

Simone's eyes widened, a panicked emotion covering her face.

"No, don't call him."

The sheriff extended a hand. "To the station with you. Your father can pick you up."

Chin lifted, Simone folded her arms over her small chest.

"Suit yourself," the sheriff said using one hand to position his hat on his head. "Autumn, follow us down to the station."

Justice was served, -wait, she must have misheard him.

"What? Why?" Autumn rebelled, diplomacy out the window. She supported the democratic process, let every voice be heard, but not if it took another second out of her day. Her landlord had given her until this morning to catch up her late payment. A child's prank was the least of her worries. Autumn had rent to pay.

The sheriff looked at her. "A dozen people heard Simone screaming you tried to take her."

"It's my car," Autumn exclaimed, not believing the entire situation. "I have class in like...thirty minutes."

Without a word, the law enforcement officer pushed past her and picked Simone up off her feet, not stopping when she squealed.

"I'll phone your dad from the station," the sheriff commented as if this were a routine occurrence.

"My daddy doesn't care. Don't call him," Simone whined, tears gathering in her eyes.

For the first time since this very bizarre exchange, Simone's expression was that of a sad little girl. Remembering all the times she'd felt unwanted, Autumn knew she would stay to see who this kid's father was. No child, not even a car-jacking, sharp-tongued miscreant should be neglected by her parent. Simone's father, whoever he was, would get a big piece of her mind.

DISAPPOINTED WITH HIMSELF, Rui Conners dropped the cordless phone back in the cradle on his oak desk. Why did he allow this pseudo-love affair to continue? Kirsten enjoyed toying with his emotions. During this morning's phone call, she'd cooed how much she missed *him*. Not him as her husband, no-she missed their lovemaking. The next woman in his life had to be head-over-heels devoted to him and Simone, to family. Until then, the question remained. How long would he welcome his ex-wife into his bed?

After three years of marriage, Kirsten had asked for a divorce. The only wedding vow she'd wanted to continue—to love him with her body and soul. Following the dissolution of his happy union, Rui had been focused on caring for their daughter, Simone and obtaining a tenured position at the university. Kirsten had poured her energy into a solo recording artist career abroad. Initially, he'd been hopeful that the intimate connections would lead to a reunion of his family. The every six months conjugal visits crept up to nine, and then twelve, now- though they still talked at least once every other day, it had been eighteen months since Kirsten's last visit. Rui wanted his life back, and Simone needed her mother.

Though he hated to admit defeat, Simone's behavior had spiraled out of control. Glancing at the Tag Heuer watch circling his wrist, he grimaced. Rui pushed to his feet, the weight of the world pressing on his shoulders. He had a class of thirty students eager to learn Asian history. If he left now, he'd arrive on campus with enough time to make his first class. Frustrated, he slid a hand into his trouser pocket as he turned in the direction of the garage. In mid-stride he paused.

Where were his keys? Turning back, he pushed papers across his office desk, patting the surface beneath. Not here. In the kitchen now, he shifted empty takeout containers from the No Limits Bar and Grille, stacks of food-crusted plates, and the towels he'd washed last night. Not here.

He glanced at the authentic Heberstein Black Forest cuckoo clock Kirsten had sent from Cologne Germany. It had been a gift their first year of marriage and his wife's second tour as a solo artist. He'd staved off loneliness by focusing on Simone. Tears had sprung to his eyes when the package had arrived at their Endurance home. The note inside read, *I'm counting the minutes until we can be together again.* That had been seven years ago, before the divorce and the lawyers. Rui shook off his melancholy, Kirsten would come to her senses and come home to them. She had to.

Crash.

Something hit the floor, and Rui winced. Peering over the counter, his breath caught when he saw the shattered picture frame. A crack in the glass spider-webbed across the photo of a younger version of him and Kirsten. Smiling, she stared lovingly down at the baby in her arms. He recalled how proud he'd been of the family he'd created. He swallowed the bitter taste that rose in his mouth. Idealistic fool. Now, her frozen smile mocked him. He and Kirsten had moved from Sacramento to Endurance to raise their family. A family they didn't have at the beginning of their marriage. Simone, his little angel, had arrived twelve months after their wedding. Rui's life was made complete that day. He had the wife, the baby, and his budding career at the University of California, Endurance.

Then, it was snatched from his grasp by a threat he'd encouraged with open arms. His phone alarm blared. Great, he had the phone, but where were his keys?

Rui ran a hand over his face, taking in the mess surrounding him. How had things gotten so out of control? Frustrated, he kicked the still full grocery bag at his feet. The tinkle of metal keys and the rhythmic roll of canned goods on a smooth surface echoed through the quiet room.

Bending, Rui scooped up his keys, grabbed his leather briefcase, and sprinted for the door.

Hand on the garage opener, he pressed the over-sized square button. Once behind the wheel, he breathed a sigh of relief. Fifteen minutes to spare. Of late, it seemed that his eight-year-old pride and joy was on a bit of a hamster wheel. Since Simone entered grade school, it had been increasingly difficult to manage himself and subsequently her. He realized he needed help, but a part of him held out hope that Kirsten would want to be a part of their lives.

Rui hit Bragg Road at thirty-five miles per hour, cruising past the Abel Burney golf course. The university was on the west side of the town center. With the craziness of the morning behind him, Rui committed to making today a good day.

His cell phone buzzed. Pressing the Bluetooth speaker link, he spoke.

"Professor Conners here." Please let it not be the dean of the college again. It seemed someone on staff had reported that Simone had been present several times during his lectures. As a single parent in a small town, he struggled to find reliable childcare and had considered hiring a live-in nanny. But, the thought of another woman in Kirsten's house unsettled him. Seemed too permanent.

"Rui, it's me."

Rui's heart clenched. Not again. Even though Endurance was small enough that he knew a significant number of the townsfolk, recognizing the sheriff's voice before he gave his name was a disturbing sign.

"What now?" Teaching was the one thing he excelled at. God knew he'd failed at his job as a husband. Truthfully, he didn't think he was doing that well as a father, either. Yesterday, Kate Glatt, the principal at Simone's elementary school, called to ask after Simone's welfare considering she'd missed school twice in the past week. Rui wasn't good with women, not even the ones under eighteen.

"Seems Simone tried to commandeer a vehicle this morning. Need you to come down to the station. The woman who owns the car looks pretty feisty. I'd come quick."

Alarm registered. "Is Simone safe?"

Keith grunted as if the question irritated him. "She's fine. Now, get here before one of my squad cars goes missing."

Rui's fingers tightened on the steering wheel. "I have a class in twenty minutes."

"And the station is not a babysitter, Rui." The line went dead.

Assured that Simone was unharmed, the clamp around his chest loosened, but not by much. Sheriff Fullerton needed him at the station to settle an incident involving Simone, a car, and a feisty woman. The sheriff's department, located in the

Endurance town square, was thirty minutes away, but his Asian studies class started in twenty. This was Simone's fourth run-in with the sheriff this school year. He needed a freaking third hand and another set of eyes to keep vigil over his daughter. He needed someone full-time to care for Simone. Just until Kirsten's next visit. They would sit down as parents and come up with a workable solution for raising a healthy, well-adjusted child.

Rui ignored the pang in his heart. He wanted his family back; his wife and daughter in a home that he as the man of the house provided for them. This equaled a family. He and Simone hadn't experienced a sense of home in a long time. He told Kirsten he'd wait forever. He still waited. She and Simone, his family, were worth the sacrifice of time. Just then, Autumn Raine's warm smile and lush curves materialized in his mind. The woman had to be the sweetest temptation in the whole state of California. He stopped the direction of his thoughts. Turning onto Saratoga Springs Road, Rui repeated his commitment; no distractions were permitted. He'd lost the life he planned with Kirsten. He refused to lose his daughter too.

CHAPTER TWO

The sweat chilling her skin did little to cool Autumn's temper. Once at the Endurance sheriff's department, they were deposited into two hard plastic chairs without an ounce of give in front of a blank-faced older woman whose eyes deterred the urge to ask a question. Like, how much longer it this going to take? Imagine if she had committed a crime, she'd need a bed and pajamas. The deputy had her driver's license and proof that the car was registered to her. Though it was obvious the vehicle belonged to her, there was still the question of Simone's would-be kidnapping. Autumn tried not to let her anger show at the ridiculous process and failed. The receptionist, sympathetic to her plight, offered her a small cup filled with lukewarm coffee. Autumn sipped the brew in gratitude, appreciative of the distraction. The office buzzed with county staff and harried citizens. People streamed back and forth behind a large window giving a full view of a large room chock full of short beige cubicles. The receptionist wasn't much of a gatekeeper considering visitors could see who was at their desk without conferring with the woman. Placing the paper coffee cup on the empty seat to their right, Autumn reached overhead, stretching her arm muscles and those lining her upper back. There was an audible release when her back peeled away from the plastic, like cellophane ripped off of CD case. Not only was she sticky from her run, she was going to be late to class. Unfortunately for her, class size at UC Endurance was small enough that everyone turned around and gawked whenever someone entered the class late. Great, now she'd have to deal with her professor's censure. She stared down at the pint-sized troublemaker seated next to her.

"You happy now?"

The kid had enough sense to looked chagrinned.

"Nope. My dad's going to ground me for a medieval century."

Autumn raised a brow. "That strict, huh?"

Simone sighed, rubbing at her reddening eyes. "Only when I get into trouble."

Autumn had the feeling Simone created more than her fair share of trouble. She imagined that for this rambunctious eight-year-old, limiting her for even an hour would translate into eternity.

"Don't worry," Autumn reassured. "I'm sure he'll go easy on you," she lied. If Simone were her daughter, she'd see sunshine when the good Lord came and rolled the stone away from her bedroom door.

"Will you talk to him?" she asked, eyes wide in earnest.

Was this kid for real? It was her decision to shanghai the car that got them both into this hump day mess. Autumn couldn't recall the last time she'd had such a terrible Wednesday.

Frowning, she draped a matronly arm over Simone's shoulders. "My closing argument would not help your case."

Simone's shoulders slumped. "Yep...I figured."

The door behind Autumn flew open.

"Simone," a man's concerned voice rang out.

The man's voice was warm apple cider on a chilly fall night. A tingle skittered down Autumn's spine. The sound was deep and firm, yet tender. His voice filtered through to all of her unmet needs and rejection; a place where she hid behind a ready smile and eager helping hands. This reckless, imagination-wielding, precocious child had a father who came for her. And then a lone figure, lean and approaching fast, strode through vast space pulling her vision into a tunnel the closer he got.

It was Rui, the professor from the history department. He strode past Autumn coming to a stop in front of Simone.

Rui Conners, with his inky black hair and matching goatee, strode right past her to wrap his little girl in a bear hug.

Honest, she tried not to make the comparison. Something had to be wrong with Autumn. Her father never came for her. Quickly, she pushed away the rejection, the sadness of an unwanted little girl tangled up in the woman she was desperately trying to become.

On her feet, the little hellion seemed to shrink before Rui's ample height. All broad shouldered with long legs and narrow hips, Autumn admired his athletic build. His skin, fairer than her soft caramel, was a light olive with the rugged lines expected from spending time in the California sun. His eyes, onyx black like his hair and framed by straight sweeping lashes, captured her attention. His almond shaped eyes lifted at the corners with a gentle sloped that hinted of his Asian ancestry. Women paid high-end private clinics for his exotic features.

"You okay?" he asked, directing the question to his daughter.

Genuine concern creased his smooth features as he took a visual stock of his offspring from head to toe. Autumn observed the entire encounter in rapt attention. Rui Conners had always appeared so mild-mannered when she saw him on campus. The School of Arts & Music building shared a campus building with the history department. Something about his quiet strength appealed to her. To see him with his daughter reinforced what she'd observed during his infrequent visits to the No Limit Bar & Grille. He stopped in No Limit some mornings, but he kept his conversation to the men folk. Now he moved with purpose, focused on what had brought him to the sheriff's office on a Wednesday morning, his daughter.

"Rui," the sheriff called from the open door of the bullpen. "Simone decided to commandeer Miss Raine's car."

The child sprang to her feet. "Did not. I hadn't even driven it, yet."

Rui gave her a quelling look. "No talking, Simone," he ordered, and the child immediately piped down.

Yes, Autumn thought. This is what responsible parenting looked like. Unlike her mother, who'd deposited Autumn with her maternal aunt for months at a time. This father cared enough to one, stick around, and two, listen even though it was obvious his kid had skipped school.

The sheriff stood near the reception area, arms crossed over his chest. "This is the third time in nine months. Maybe some counseling would help."

At the mention of professional intervention, Autumn saw the immediate change in father and child.

"I can take care of my own child, sheriff."

Autumn's heart ached for this family. She wondered what had happened to make the child behave in such a manner? Children like Simone, troubled or troublesome, were the reason Autumn had chosen a career that merged her two passions, music and counseling. Her junior high school counselor, Mr. Locklayer, had loved jazz. She'd noticed the music piped in through invisible speakers the first time she'd visited his office. After a few months, he began explaining each section of the piece and educating her about the art form and the artists. He played a new piece every time she came for a session. Pretty soon, he was mentoring her, not just in music, but through her difficult home situation.

It was none of her business, but Rui seemed like a good father. He'd have some stiff words for his daughter. She hoped Simone appreciated her father's presence in her life. Autumn had only seen her father once. It had been by accident. She'd come home from school early to hear a man's voice, harsh and demeaning. Tears streamed down her mother's face as she begged him to stay, to love her. She promised she'd do whatever he wanted, but he'd left moments later. It was the first and last time Autumn saw the stranger who'd given her life. A week later, her mom had dropped Autumn, one suitcase, and twenty dollars at her aunt's one-bedroom apartment in Chula Vista. She'd been nine. Seventeen years later and here she was, that same unwanted little girl, trying to find a place to fit in.

Rui's face was kind, but stern as he regarded his child. Hard to believe this little goddess of mischief had a father as compassionate and kind-hearted as Professor Rui Conners.

The sight of Rui pulling his daughter in for an embrace tugged at her heartstrings. The child instantly rested her head on her father's shoulder, clinging like Scarlett O'Hara to the last turnip on a desolate southern plantation. It was then that Autumn noticed the satisfied gleam in Simone's eyes.

The sheriff stood watching from beyond the glass, a frown on his face, shaking his head.

Realization dawned. This kid had her father wrapped around her finger. All the soft edges that Autumn felt toward this pair dropped like a bowling ball.

Autumn opened her mouth, prepared to strike this dynamic duo right between the eyes. Rui Conners needed a swift kick to the backside if he fell for this theatrical production.

Then he looked at her. "Forgive me for being so rude. I was so worried about my daughter...and you. Are you okay, Autumn?"

He knew her name. Dear angel of secret crushes, the sexiest professor on campus had stared deep into Autumn's eyes and uttered her name. Everything inside her froze.

"It is, Autumn, right? Your name," Rui asked. "Did I get it wrong?"

Nope. Autumn don't do it, she chided herself. Not under any circumstances is it okay to let this adult male off the hook for his child's behavior. Give him a piece of flaming hot junior-college educated mind. His daughter had wrecked her morning routine, and now she was about to be late for class. Regarding the rent, she'd ask the Tate's for a loan. Hopefully, Ivy would agree if Autumn promised to repay the money.

She met his gaze boldly, and then narrowed her eyes. "Yes, my name is Autumn. And it's about time...,"

To her annoyance he smiled, "It's nice to finally meet you, Autumn,"

A funny thing happened. All that junior-college witty comeback stuff slipped right out of her head.

RUI would've recognized Autumn, even with the wide-eyed expression on her face. He'd memorized every detail of her features. With her expressive brown eyes, she was the most exquisite creature Rui had seen in years. The first time he'd spotted her sweetheart face had been on campus, maybe eight months ago. Since then the sexy sitter had been making random pop-ups, like those pesky websites fishing for his email address for some newsletter subscription. Ignore her he told himself, but at least twice a week he'd walk through the doors of No Limit hoping to get a glimpse of her. In the last few months she'd been scarce around the bar, but on the rare occasion when their eyes had met, hers shot fire in his direction.

He regarded her.

Shorter than his six feet by a several inches, Autumn was all toned curves, bright smiles, and sandy brown natural curls. His heart started to pitter-patter. A thin dry-weave tank clung to her small chest, outlining her twin mounds. The fluorescent green fabric hung damp over her flat abdomen, sticking in places. Rui wished she wore a garbage bag dress and a mop bucket hat, it would be less distracting than seeing the sleek outline of her body. Toned thighs and calves filled out her stretchy dark blue and fluorescent green leggings. Matching running shoes with a familiar swoosh logo adorned her feet.

How could he have missed her standing so close, breathing in the same air entering his lungs? The tight line formed by her full fall berry-colored lips indicated he'd upset her. Honestly, he looked forward to whatever she wanted to throw at him, but...duty called. So, Rui did something he rarely did when dealing with women, he finished her thought.

"It's time for us to go."

Her pregnant pause morphed into hands bare of nail color planted on her round curves. "Well, that's just great. Simone tries to steal my car and I am the one stuck without a ride."

Well, that he could fix.

"Come with us," he offered.

She did the cutest little double blink before wrinkling her slightly upturned nose. Had he surprised her?

"You'll have to take me to my car."

The request was delivered with caution as if he would refuse. Rui had no doubt Simone had instigated whatever happened involving the car. Considering his daughter's antics had served as the catalyst, of course, he would take Autumn back to her - wait... Rui looked over her head to the plain-faced clock over the entrance door. Five minutes to class time.

"We have to get Simone to school, and then on to the university."

"But,"

"Why do we have to give her a ride?" Simone protested. "She was running when I met her."

Rui gritted his teeth, embarrassed by his daughter's blatant disregard for her role in Autumn's predicament.

He cut her off before she could say more.

"Perhaps, you'd like to join her since you entered her car without permission."

Now both females shot fiery darts at his head.

To Autumn he said. "I promise I'll take care of whatever you need after Simone is in class."

She'd probably walk away now. Seemed everything he did drove women running in the opposite direction. Even during his marriage, Kirsten invented ways to stay away.

"My class starts at nine-forty, too. You won't make it in time."

Rui waved a hand at Keith and then escorted his precious cargo outside. Autumn sat next to him, a soft smile on her face. He could hardly believe his luck. He'd dreamt of ways to strike up a conversation since her arrival in town. Now she occupied the normally vacant spot next to him.

"All buckled in?" he asked, just wanting to hear her voice.

With a slight tilt of her head, Autumn gave a nod. "Yes, sure am," she said, giving the seat beat little tug.

Simone wore her headphones in the backseat, so she didn't respond. His daughter loved her music. Just like..., he stopped himself from expounding on the thought. Instead, he focused on Autumn. This beautiful woman had maintained her cool while he handled things at the sheriff's office. It made him admire her more. Rui wanted to know everything about her: the foods she liked, the type of places she visited, what brought her to Endurance. There were a lot of men in town, many of them single fathers like him. Maybe, she was looking for a husband. He had a gut feeling that Autumn Raine would be a good wife, one who would honor her commitments.

"Then we're off," he replied.

Rui would raise his daughter to honor her commitments, education, family, and marriage. Growing up the son of a statesman, Rui had spent a significant portion of his childhood abroad. His father, a Virginia farm boy with a master's degree in International Policy, had met his mother, a Hong Kongese administrative assistant, during a two-year assignment as consulate general. After marrying, Zhen Conners had become a full-time wife and mother, dedicated to caring for her child and building a solid marriage. Thirty-four years together and his parents were still very much in love.

Foolhardy, when Rui met Kirsten he'd believed most women wanted the life his mother had. Simone would not be like her mother. She wasn't. Yet, when he looked at her, Kirsten had stamped her DNA on every part of their child. He blew out a breath. Simone's antics had disrupted their lives and others more in the past twelve months than all her eight years. He'd asked his daughter if anything was wrong, but she denied anyone bullying her at school. He knew that the kids teased her about not having a mother. He tried to be available as much as possible, but he had a full-time schedule at the university. There was no way he could cut back on his hours. He had a mortgage, a car payment, a college fund, music lessons, and gymnastics would start next month. Again, he needed three hands. A nanny would help, but Rui admitted that his daughter could tempt a holy man to abandon his religion.

"I'm sorry about Simone. She's having an elementary-school crisis."

Autumn smiled at that. "Sounds worse than mid-life."

Another reality check. At thirty-one, Rui wondered if love had completely bypassed him. He believed Kirsten would come back home, but...would he settle for a woman who couldn't commit to her own child? Early on in her tour, he and a then infant Simone had made the fourteen-hour flight to Dublin. Kirsten's life was so much faster: more lights, more cameras, more action, more men. They loved her; the audience, her crew, her manager. She'd assured him their marriage was rock-solid, but so were the divorce papers he'd received twelve months later.

"You should call your teacher's assistant," Autumn suggested. "He or she."

"He," he offered, not wanting her to think there was another woman in his inner circle. She dipped her head in acknowledgement.

"He," she parroted, "could start the class until you arrived."

Why hadn't he thought of that? His head was in the clouds. Better than being up his-

"I like you already, Autumn Raine." He loved the smile that spread across her face at the miniscule compliment. He would have to give a few more words of affirmation before she left him.

"I don't," Simone mumbled from the black seat.

Looking over his shoulder, he shot his daughter a stern look. To which, she promptly rolled her eyes. God in heaven, he needed to pray for more patience. Simone's behavior went way beyond troubling this morning. What had changed to trigger this open defiance? He needed to spend some time with Simone and get to the bottom of what was troubling her.

Turning to Autumn, he said, "I apologize."

He sounded like a thirty-three-inch record single stuck on stupid.

Autumn waved him off with an understanding heart. "It's not your fault."

Of course it was. Simone's behavior was a direct reflection on him as a parent. He appreciated Autumn's attempt to spare his feelings. It made Rui like her even more. He made the call to his assistant.

"Glenn," he spoke through the Bluetooth link after it connected. "Please, start the class. You'll find the exam in the electronic file." He listened, offering the expected yes and hum. Ten minutes passed before he could get Glenn off the phone. Done with that, he whizzed through town and took a sharp right turn onto Saratoga Springs Road. Endurance Elementary sat across from Tommy's Park on Kings Bay Drive. The park ran along the back side of Owen Tate's No Limit Bar & Grille. On occasion he would stop by the bar for one of Ivy Summer's home cooked meals to-go. It was easy to do since he had to pick Simone up from school by four o'clock.

"So, how long have you been in Endurance?"

Autumn turned from the window to face him.

"About eight months. Do you mind turning on some music?"

So, he'd been right. She was relatively new in town.

Rui gestured to the center console. "I have Sirius radio. Pick your poison. So, you like it here?"

She laughed. "Of course, Professor. I picked the place."

He chuckled, realizing how crazy the question must seem to her. "Sorry. Usually I'm a better listener."

After tuning-in to Sirius Love songs, she placed a hand over his where it rested on the gear shift. Rui prayed the voice that haunted his sleep didn't start up.

"No worries," she said, a furrow pulling her brows low. "It's been a rough start for me, too."

Now, why did he get the distinct impression that she referred to more than the run-in with Simone? He wanted to bring a smile to her face.

"Well," he said stroking his thumb over her knuckles. "I'll do what I can to make your day better."

"Can you explain to my teacher why I missed class."

Easy peasy. "Yes."

Knowing that she wasn't angry about missing class eased his mind. For some reason, he didn't want her to see him as a failure. It was obvious he had some struggles with Simone, but all kids had their challenges at some point. Simone was an early bloomer in the trouble department.

Rui parked in front of the school, careful not to block the red zoned fire lane. Before he could round the car, Simone hopped out.

"Sweetie," he called after her.

"Mr. Conners."

Rui clenched at the sound of the principal's voice. The woman's tone was something between nails on a chalkboard and a rusted bike chain. In a word, painful.

"Yes, ma'am," he said looking up.

Without preamble, the matronly woman cupped Simone on the shoulder and held on.

"This is the third time this month that Simone has been absent, and I use the term loosely," she said, lifting her pug-like nose. "Here at Endurance Elementary, we take truancy as a serious parenting issue."

"Who you calling a truant?" Simone shot back.

Rui bristled at the thinly-veiled insult. Cutting his eyes at his daughter, he lifted a finger. "That's enough, Simone."

He didn't like to take that tone with his child. In front of the principal and within hearing shot of Autumn, he thought they might consider him a bully. It was important to Rui that Autumn knew the type of man he was: protective, a provider, a competent man at work and at home. Simone's recent defiance challenged more than his authority; it compounded his doubts about himself as a father.

"I apologize that she's tardy."

The principal held up a palm. "Save it, Mr. Conners. I heard from a reliable source that Simone was involved in a police matter."

Rui bit his tongue. One of the disadvantages of a small town; everyone talked too much. "If she's late or has an unexcused absence again this semester, I will have no other choice but to expel Simone for the remainder of the school year."

His temper ignited. "The year," he gritted out. "Now, wait a minute."

A hand threading though his elbow and then holding on tight stopped him. He looked to his left to find Autumn at his side. That smile of hers was lit up like a Sacramento night club.

She took over since he was rendered speechless. "We understand," Autumn interjected. "Simone will be on time from here on out."

The woman studied Autumn, taking in her features and manor of dress. Rui could tell neither of them passed the principal's muster.

"Are you the child's mother?"

At the question, Rui looked to his daughter. A flash of pain sparked behind his little one's eyes, before he saw the defiance pull her spine straighter, a blank mask slipping into place. This was one of the reasons why he had objected to Keith's suggestion of mental health services. Never would he want Simone to bare the stigma associated with seeking psychiatric services because his ex-wife was self-serving and irresponsible. His daughter would not suffer for his mistake. Rui had picked the wrong woman. Damn Kirsten for hurting their child this way.

A few of Rui's fondest childhood memories materialized and a wall of sadness nearly crushed him. Where he had memories of being held in his mother's arms, splashing around at the beach, running in the park-Simone only had photographs. Kirsten had relegated him to stud status in her life. He'd trained himself to ignore that injustice, but he still struggled to accept that she had walked away from her own flesh and blood.

"I'm here," Autumn said, her tone communicating that she would not be answering anymore questions. "And, she won't be late again."

She walked over and hugged Simone. "Have a great day at school, sweetie."

His little girl stood as rigid as he did. Who was this kick-ass woman?

"Humph," the principal said, before taking a still shocked Simone by the arm and leading her behind the locked gate.

Rui swallowed, and then asked. "So, you're going to take on getting Simone to...."

Her reply came like lightning. "No. Your daughter almost had me arrested like an hour ago, dude." She laughed.

"Yeah," Rui said, rubbing his big hands over his goatee "there is that," he smiled. "Then why charge in like a crusader with Mrs. Glatt?"

Curiosity had him anxious for her reply.

"I remember having teachers like that woman. No kid deserves to be made to feel like they're lacking something. Adults can be cruel."

Though she tried to keep the pain out of her voice, Rui heard all the cuts and bruises behind the admission.

"So, can children," he said, studying her. At one time had she reacted like Simone, back straight with an impenetrable mask, feeling like a spotlight shone on her for everyone to gawk? After he dropped Autumn off, he and Mrs. Glatt needed to set some boundaries. He would not tolerate anyone targeting Simone. She needed guidance more than censure.

Rui reached across the console and grabbed Autumn's hand. He wondered who'd hurt this courageous and beautiful woman? Whatever she lacked, he wanted to provide. Now, where had that thought come from?

CHAPTER THREE

After listening to that judgmental principal denigrate Rui and Simone, Autumn's gut twisted into a knot. She remembered it happening to her more times than she could count. Her aunt, often times agreed with the teachers, so Autumn stood alone in her condemnation. A little girl with no mother, no father, isolated and powerless against her attackers. Even now, the pain of her childhood stung like a fresh cut. As a child, she'd gone out of her way to be quiet, respectful and friendly, to help out, and to share the little she had. Her sacrifices seemed to keep some of the criticism at bay. Well, mostly. The kids still teased her, the bullies still pushed her, knowing she had no savior to come to her defense. No sleepovers, no party invites, no prom date. Autumn Raine was doomed to spend her life alone. For now, at least.

When she won the 100K run and the $75,000 scholarship, people would remember her name. With her bachelor's degree in music therapy, she'd teach children how to heal. Hopefully with the application of music improvisation and therapeutic communication they could build healthier lives. Had she healed? Some days she thought she had, others, she knew she'd just found better ways to hide her wounds. Whenever she saw another kid being marginalized for a life they never chose, she'd befriend them. Funny, it wasn't until high school that she realized few people had been a friend to her. Autumn was like an invisible force field, taking blows meant for others, only to be discarded when they didn't need her any longer.

"Hey," Rui's voice cut through her morbid past. "Penny for your thoughts."

She smiled at him. "I need at least a dollar." She laughed.

When he just studied her, she broke eye contact beneath his watchful stare. "That was a joke."

He looked back at the road. "Really?"

Nope.

"Of course." She laughed it off.

His comment sobered her. She needed to get to her car, and then over to No Limit. Autumn was sure Owen would loan her the money to cover a part of her rent. She'd fallen behind when her car needed a new alternator. Her aunt had "blessed" her with the Millennium Falcon of cars, so the thing was held together with junkyard parts, an angel wing, and lots of prayer.

"I promised to get you to campus, but class will be over before I get through the mid-morning rush in town."

"I know. My car isn't far from here. Just on the other side of Smitty's Watering hole at the park."

He nodded and eased back up Kings Bay Drive.

"So, you run around the lake?"

Talking about running relaxed her. Autumn wasn't a natural athlete. She had to psyche herself up every morning, the music pumping through her earbuds helped. Knowing if she failed at this, she'd have nothing. She had no real accomplishments outside of completing high school and her two-year degree in special education. She'd been so excited until she learned the piece of paper got her little more than a teacher's aide position or a minimum wage daycare worker slot. She'd tried both, but the pay barely covered her bills without much left for savings.

"I'm training for the Western America 100-mile race," she beamed. "I'm going to win that $75,000 first prize." Maybe if she said it enough she would believe it.

Rui hit the steering wheel with one hand. "Wow, that's impressive."

"You think so?" she asked. Was he mocking her? Her aspirations for completing a bachelor's degree probably seemed minuscule compared to a doctoral-prepared professor.

"Heck, ya. You're a real-life celebrity."

They passed the empty stands for the Farmers Market. Hood Road was mainly residential, so there weren't many cars on the street. Tommy's Park would be hopping by mid-afternoon with stroller moms and senior citizens. For now, the parking lot held only her vehicle. "That's me," she said pointing ahead.

Rui pulled in next to her and put the car in park.

"Thanks for being so understanding about Simone. I'm really sorry."

She was about to say no problem, but it had been a major problem.

"Please, stop apologizing, Rui. I may not have kids of my own, but I understand they have a mind of their own. I'll figure it out."

Hopefully. She'd lost two hours of her morning and she still needed to talk with Owen about the money. Her landlord had grown impatient with her partial payments. Autumn tried to make up for the short falls by sharing her meals, cutting the grass with a hand-powered mower. One weekend, she'd even gotten a can of paint from the garage, repainted the fence.

"Just taking responsibility for my own."

"Yeah, there's definitely a country song in there," Autumn teased. She expected him to laugh. Instead, a pinched expression crossed his face and then it was gone.

"I'll wait and follow you out."

Opening the door, she reassured him, "There's no need, Rui. I'll be fine." With that, Autumn waved good-bye and walked to her car.

Behind the wheel of her vintage Beetle, she stuck the key in the ignition, and turned. Nothing. She wiggled the key and tried again. Rui sat patiently, waiting. No, no, no. This could not be happening to her. Please let him leave. With her right foot, she pumped the gas pedal three times while she twisted the key. Nope, nada, nothing. Giving a deep exhale, she closed her eyes, searching for the calm to slow her racing heart. She didn't have the money for a tow truck and she didn't need him to see her make the run back home.

Leaning over she reached for the window handle and cranked the squeaky glass down. She ignored the fact that the angular pane had slipped off its track. To fix it, she'd have to exit the car, and then use both hands to pull the thick plate of glass back into place.

"You can go." Please. If the car started, it rattled worse than a tin can on asphalt. She preferred not to have an audience when that happened.

To Autumn's dismay, Rui got out of the car. Great.

Bending, he peered into the window. "What's wrong?"

Heck if she knew. She'd replaced everything on the car, but the candy shell. Thank goodness, the paint job could wait a few years, at least until after graduation.

"Putter is just being temperamental," she offered, hoping her lighthearted reply would cut back on his questions.

He stuck his head through the open window. Whoa, his hair shone like black gold. In that moment, she wondered what it would feel like to run her fingers through his thick mane.

"You named your car, Putter?"

A soft smile spread across his lips. Autumn thought he looked younger in that moment. There always seemed to be an edge of anxiety surrounding Rui Connors whenever she passed him in the campus breezeways.

She shrugged. "As evidenced by her behavior, the name fits."

Stupid piece of junk would cost her money she didn't have.

"Pop the hood," he said, moving in front of the car.

She frowned. Everyone knew the classic Beetle engine was in the rear of the car.

"Hey, professor."

"Yeah? Please call me Rui," he called back. "You're not one of my students."

A small miracle, too. Not a word he uttered would stick in her head because she'd be too busy staring at his handsome face.

"Engine's in the back."

He looked up, cheeks reddening. "I knew that."

Jogging past her window, she heard his laughter.

Ten minutes passed. Nothing. Another ten. Nada. Okay, men didn't like to be bothered when they were tinkering but shouldn't he have said something.

The creak of the heavy metal door opening alerted him to her arrival.

"Everything okay?" Autumn asked.

Lifting his head from the engine block, gave he a sheepish grin. She frowned.

"What?" she squeaked, afraid the repairs would bankrupt her.

He briefly looked away as if he was leery to share his thoughts.

"I don't know a thing about cars," he confessed. "And," he said rubbing his neck and spreading engine crud on his skin, "this one is more confusing than most. Literally, this engine with all these little hoses crammed together reminds me of a balled-up term paper."

Her eyes stretched wide in amazement. "So, you've been back here posing for the last ten minutes?" She couldn't contain her laughter.

He shrugged. "Well, I thought something might look familiar."

"Oh, sugar plum fairy, like a little computer mouse hand flashing, click here." She laughed harder.

His chuckle was low and deep. The sound filled her with delight. She liked Rui Conners. He was an academician, not a mechanic, but she appreciated the gesture.

"Let me call a tow truck," he said rounding the side of the car, coming to stand beside her.

"No," she said too quickly.

He slammed the hood and leaned his compact backside on the slotted grill. "Why not?" Autumn knew she needed to shape her answer. Endurance was a small town. Not being able to pay her rent was a private matter. Her car sitting at Raymond's garage for weeks because of non-payment would make her financial situation very public.

Why indeed?

"I have a car repair kit at home. I can probably fix it." A half-truth. She did have some tools, one of those pink zippered numbers from the half-off after Christmas sale aisle. Autumn prayed somewhere amongst the wrench and twist-ties, she had the tools to fix it.

"Okay," he said.

She released a sigh. Now, he would leave.

"Hop in," he offered. "I'll give you a ride."

Oh, the last thing she needed was to be alone with Rui Conners.

RUI darted a glance at his passenger in rapt amusement as Autumn stuck her hands out the open sunroof and high-fived the rays of sunshine.

"Having fun?"

She giggled like Kirsten used to. Before she realized marriage to a college professor lacked the spotlight, she'd laughed at his jokes. Motherhood had been a poor substitute for fame. The combination of marriage and motherhood had robbed his wife of her joy. Looking back, it was foolish to think supporting one more tour abroad would bring his wife back to him. He'd been desperate to save his family, so he'd given his blessing, agreeing to be a single parent for one year. Stupid.

"Absolutely. I wish I had the kind of money to afford a car with a sunroof."

She fell silent, as if she'd said too much. Rui wanted her to feel comfortable confiding in him. He sought to reassure her.

"You'll have it."

Slowly, a soft smile formed across her face. "Thank you, Rui."

He thought to use this time to get to know her.

"Tell me about you, Autumn." She tried to turn away. Since they were at a traffic stop, he touched her chin and turned her face to his. "Tell me."

She shrugged. "Nothing to tell, really. To celebrate my twenty-sixth birthday, I moved here from southern California to complete my degree in music therapy. I taught myself to play the piano and guitar. In three weeks, I'll spend no more than 31 hours outrunning hundreds of ultra athletes in order to secure my future. When I'm not training or studying, I babysit Owen Tate's little boy, if he and Ivy want alone time."

Whoa, at thirty-two he felt like an old fart compared to her. He'd heard talk about town of her working on a bachelors curriculum. At Autumn's age, most students had completed their four-year degree. Could he have received misinformation?

"Sounds like you're a determined and talented young woman on a mission. How much longer before you graduate?"

She smiled. "Thanks, but I'm just getting started again. I still have another two years to complete."

Rui wondered what happened to interrupt her formal education. As the only child, his Chinese mother had drilled into his head the importance of education. Even as an elementary student, there was no accommodation in his academic calendar for friendships, recreation, social clubs, or athletics.

"And your family?" Rui wanted to know all about the people who raised this fiercely determined yet fun-loving woman.

Her smiled slipped, but she quickly pulled it back in place. "It's just me. I have an aunt down south, but..." she hesitated. "We give one another a wide berth."

Autumn grimaced as if in pain, but then that smile reappeared. Was it a wide berth or a permanent rift? Her expression led him to believe the latter.

Rui frowned. "What happened to your parents?"

She squirmed and Rui could tell by the stiff posture she was uncomfortable with his questions.

"Autumn, I didn't mean to-,"

She held up a hand. "It's fine." He knew it wasn't. "I'm not sure where they are. I saw my father once. My mother left afterwards. I think to chase after him," her voice trailed off. "Guess he was the life she wanted."

Autumn's matter-of-fact retelling surprised him. Anger swelled inside of him just listening. What must it have felt like to have a parent leave you behind chasing after a fantasy?

He said his next words with caution. "Well, that sucks."

She smiled, but Rui noticed the tension lines framing her mouth. "My aunt, my mother's younger sister, she took me in. So, I'm good." Took her in-like laundry that needed to be folded and put away in a closet? "I'm not sure why I dumped that on you."

He stroked her cheek with his thumb. "Pretty sure, I asked for it. Besides, I'm loyal. You won't hear a word on the Endurance gossip line."

Not wanting to step on another landmine, he changed the subject.

"What do you do for fun?"

She met his eyes with her gaze. "Run."

He chuckled. "I hate running, so I need to introduce you to another hobby."

Images of he and Autumn sharing a kiss, deep and passionate, came to mind. Bú *hǎo*. Not good. Burying the thought, Rui cut a quick glance at Autumn. His chest tightened at how sweet she looked, fresh. He bet she'd taste good, too.

She grinned. "Running is akin to music."

He wanted to keep asking questions just to hear her voice. "In what way?"

"A solo can be just as beautiful as a duet."

Had she spent a lot of time alone? Following his divorce, Rui had little energy to socialize. Not that he was good at small talk or non-academic conversations, but the fact that he no longer belonged to anyone magnified how alone he'd always been.

"What else?"

"Let's see, there's eating, running, working or job-hunting, sleeping, and-,"

"Wait a minute," Rui cut in, "those are all necessities."

"I'm a college student on a partial scholarship. I'm trying to avoid the six-figure student loan trap, so I sacrifice."

He didn't mean his question to sound insensitive or out of touch. His father's Montgomery GI bill had covered the education costs beyond the four-year scholarship he received.

With the car in motion, he kept his eyes on the road. "Sorry if I was being critical."

When he felt a hand settle on his forearm he relaxed. "It's fine, Rui. And you're right, sometimes I hang out at Diego's. I memorize chord shapes, note values, and time signatures when they have live musicians."

He looked at her. "I don't think I've ever heard any of those words used together. Chord shapes?"

She smiled that smile again, and his pulse sped up.

When they passed Abel Burney's golf course, he frowned. Where was her place? The countryside opened up once he passed the driving range. Nothing much beyond Abel's place except open fields and the highway. The private homes were few and miles apart.

"How did you find your place?" he asked. Endurance, though small, it was impossible to know every road. Lots of folks kept to themselves, drank well water, ate what they grew and hunted. He kept close to town or the campus, so he didn't know many of the farmers.

She chuckled. "Went for the cheapest place advertised, and then finagled an additional one-hundred off the asking price."

"Seems quiet," he said. In truth the road looked deserted. He wondered how safe it was for a woman alone. This area of Endurance was miles away from town which was twenty miles from the campus.

"Too quiet sometimes. But between school and work, I'm not home often."

"How many jobs do you have?"

She cut her eyes. "You're mighty inquisitive, Professor Conners."

He felt warmth heat his face. "Sorry, I have an eight-year-old, so my filters are pretty much null and void."

A hearty laugh filled the car. "I get it. Cai keeps asking to taste me like I'm a piece of chocolate."

Rui totally understood the boy's fascination.

"Oh, there's the turn," she said pointing to an unpaved road he would've missed without her direction. "Turn between those two rusted out mailboxes."

"Where?" Rui asked, searching the roadside.

Sure enough, two breadbox style boxes with red tin molded into miniatures flags mounted on a thick wooden beam came into view.

Slowly Rui left the smooth tar of the highway, for the crunch of gravel beneath his tires. The road could double as an office building hallway. Rui could hear the sweep of the overgrown bush against his paint job. The sedan dipped, and the underbelly scraped on the gravel road. He winced when the car bounced and juggled over one pot-hole after another, the sound was as coarse as metal in a blender. Seriously, no wonder Autumn's car was falling apart. This road was the worst.

They pulled up in front of a tiny two-story structure. A stout man with a dingy white wife beater under a plaid long-sleeved shirt worked at stacking boxes in the driveway. He continued to pile colorful crates and cardboard containers on the curb.

A strangled sound came for Rui's passenger seat. He looked over. Autumn's eyes were fixed on the pile of trash the man heaped higher with each box. Tears streamed down her face. What the hell was happening?

"I thought I had more time," he heard her whisper.

By her stark expression, Rui knew what the scene before them represented. The ever-increasing pile of boxes contained Autumn's belongings. She was being evicted.

"Autumn," he said cautiously. She looked so fragile, a different person from the one who'd come to his daughter's rescue with Mrs. Glatt. His heart pounded in his chest. He found himself wanting to scoop her up in his arms, protect her.

"Please, Rui." Her lip trembled. "Please, don't tell anyone."

They needed to get something straight from the start. He took her fingers in his own, surprised by how cold they felt against his skin. He didn't get a reaction. That made him nervous.

"Hey." He shook her hand. "Come on little tigress, eyes on me."

She sat perfectly still, the confident woman on a full retreat. Rui needed to reach her, but how? He trapped her chin between his thumb and forefinger. Closing the distance between them, he placed a chaste kiss to the corner of her mouth.

"It's okay," he whispered, hoping his touch was a comfort. Though he knew little about Autumn, he felt confident in his statement. Later if things ran more amuck, he'd do what he could to make it better for her.

She angled her head, her lips parting. Her vulnerability undid him. A part of him registered that this was wrong, but in this moment, she needed him. Everything in Rui wanted to meet that need. So, he covered her mouth with his, all the while using his thumbs to wipe away the tears that continued to flow. The kiss was tender and juicy, her mouth, hot and delicious. Yes, Autumn was the best meal Rui had tasted in forever, and he was nowhere near being full. He was just getting started, warming to the awakening need, his fingers threading into her hair, when she stopped.

"Wow," she said pulling away.

That's exactly how Rui felt. When she looked at him, he felt connected to her. He felt-

She stared at him. "That was," what would she say-maybe perfect-, "wildly inappropriate."

Rui stammered. Not the response he was going for. Suddenly, the air conditioning seemed to be blowing hot air.

She started to laugh, almost hysterically, and then she dropped her head to his shoulder and cried.

Swallowing, he whispered, "It's going to be okay."

She shook her head. "No," she sobbed, "it's not."

"Shhh," he coaxed. "We'll figure something out."

That had her lifting her head. "Does it involve another one of your kisses?" She sniffled. "You're a great kisser, by the way."

Should he respond? Should he keep quiet? Rui was so out of his element. Maybe, he should say something.

"Thanks." That sounded dorky. God, he needed a textbook, an app, or blog on how to talk with a woman.

Autumn pushed away from him, sitting up straight in the ergonomic seat.

Instantly, he was sorry for uttering a single word that would make her withdraw from him.

Wiping her tear stained hand on her leggings, she said, "This isn't your problem, Rui."

Now, why did her trying to eliminate him grate on his protective instincts?

"Autumn let me help. I won't rest if I leave you here."

She ran a hand over her eyes in a windshield-wiper fashion. The wetness disappeared, but unshed tears brimmed in her eyes.

"Unless you can talk my landlord into bringing my belongings back inside, you should go."

"Not happening, honey. I'll take care of this." Culturally, Rui had been raised to be non-confrontational. But, a man had a responsibility to provide and protect his woman.

"Rui, you don't know me."

True, but he wanted to. He fixed her in a hard stare, his eyes dropped to her mouth. The lips he'd just kissed.

Autumn reared back. "Are going to kiss me again?"

Rui shook off his stupid gene and focused. "Not right this moment," he said truthfully. "And, we don't know each other well, but I know I'm not leaving you here to handle this alone."

Rui pulled the caddy into the single car driveway making it impossible for her landlord to unload anymore of Autumn's personal effects on the curb.

With a box under each arm, the stout troll of a man scowled at the parked car. Before he could exit the vehicle, Autumn opened the door and rushed forward.

"Please, Mr. Swinney, I'll get your money."

Unceremoniously, the man dropped his twin cargo. The sound of glass shattering crackled in the air.

"No, you won't" he bellowed. "You said that last month and the one before that."

"I know, but—"

"No more excuses, young lady. I'm done."

Autumn's tears continued, but the man seemed unaffected.

"You have till morning to move your things. I've already called bulk trash."

Her back stiffened. "That can take up to three days."

The guy had the audacity to smirk. "I called on Monday."

Like a pissed off kitten, Rui can see Autumn's invisible hackles rise.

"Why you lowdown, no-account, greasy hunk of pound cake," she retorted. When she raised a balled-up fist, Rui jumped out of the car. He grabbed Autumn around the waist, using his body to separate the two.

"Okay, okay. Let's get you out of here," he said keeping ahold of her waist.

"Yeah, crazy broad."

Rui froze. Meeting the eyes of the property manager, he took a step forward. "Don't" he growled, "ever call her anything other than her name."

The man scrambled backwards. "Who are you?" he challenged. Turning, he said, "I'm calling the cops."

Rui doubted the guy was serious, but he hustled Autumn back to the car. Within thirty minutes he had the backseat, the trunk and the space by Autumn's feet packed with boxes.

"Where should I take you?" he asked.

She gave a watery smile. "Back to Chula Vista, I guess."

He'd heard of the southern California town, close to the Interstate-5 Mexico border.

A desolate expression etched deep grooves into her forehead and bracketed her mouth. He couldn't let her leave. Today was the first time they'd shared a meaningful conversation. He wanted more. And, he thought maybe she did, too.

"You know," he started. "I could use some help with Simone and around my house." She didn't respond. "Autumn, did you hear me?"

"Sorry, what do you say?"

When she still remained silent. Rui sweetened the pie.

"It includes room and board."

She hit him with hopeful, but weary eyes. "How much does it pay?"

"I can pay you one thousand dollars a month." It wasn't much, but without having to pay rent and food maybe it could help.

She studied him. "I need to be paid weekly and...and I want the option to renegotiate my pay after the first thirty days. Also, I need time to train and study. I won't give up school."

"Agreed," he said without hesitation.

"Then you got yourself a nanny."

Rui smiled as they pulled back onto the dirt road. He wasn't sure if he'd negotiated a win-win or not, but her tears had stopped, and he felt like the luckiest man alive. Now, how would Simone react to having a woman in the house?

CHAPTER FOUR

From the moment Rui opened the garage door leading into the kitchen, Autumn knew she should've asked for more money. The first thing she noticed about her ranch-style farmhouse accommodations was the stench of the original funky chicken break dancing in one-hundred-degree heat singeing her nostrils. She stilled, covering her nose and mouth. That didn't help. Peering at the expansive kitchen, she could hardly believe her eyes.

A long rectangular wood bench table with iron trestle work and four blue and white checkered print parson chairs on one side lay hidden beneath a mountain of clothes. An icicle blue couch sat on the opposite side completing the breakfast nook. There were pizza boxes, grocery bags, dirty glasses, and empty bottles covering the butcher block wood countertops. Open cube containers like the ones from the fried chicken places sat on top of the mess. And then there were books and more books mixed in with about three months worth of envelopes on the table.

When was the last time they cleaned the place? The soft click of the door lock engaging signaled Rui would soon close the distance between them. Her eyes darted around the room. The passage to middle earth could be under all this stuff, she thought. All of a sudden, male hardness slammed into her back and she stumbled further into the room.

Rui caught her around the waist, holding her steady.

"I-ah, sorry" he stammered, "I have gotten behind on the house cleaning."

She squinted up at Rui, making sure no signs of madness shone in his eyes. Mr. Clean, the bald giant with the sparkling white pullover and equally dazzling smile, would curse Rui to hades and back if he saw this place.

Stunned she asked, "Was the place ever clean? Maybe you should drop me off at Owen's."

The man had to be crazy if he thought she would accept a thousand dollars to live in this place. Walking through the door had earned her bonus pay.

"It gets better," he said in a rush. "Let me show you the rest of the house," he said, gripping her shoulder.

Autumn wasn't sure she wanted to see more. Rui had seemed just about perfect when he offered her a job and a place to stay. Now, she was sure he got the winning end of the deal.

Rui hung a jacket she hadn't realized he carried on a peg behind the door. His hand slid down her arm to grip her fingers. They made their way across the wide plank floor into a large room. The floors were pine stained in a dark finish, and an entertainment center covered most of one wall on her left. On the far end, large windows flanked a pair of white French doors leading to an outside deck. The furniture was simple. An ash gray couch with a matching chair and love seat formed a 'u' shape in front of the huge structure holding a television large enough to view a mountain range. Odd, Rui struck her as the intellectual type. There were more books in this room, too, but the television and shelves lined with old record albums drew her attention.

Slipping her fingers from his, she moved closer to the shelves, studying the collection and a large jade dragon statue.

Touching the etched scales, the stone felt cool. Intricate details hinted at the quality of the artwork.

"Is it okay that I stroked your dragon?" she asked absently, now thumbing through vintage albums.

"Whatever makes you happy." Autumn noticed how he watched her, as if she were sweetest thing since chocolate milk. She liked his eyes on her.

"You like music?" she quizzed. He didn't seem offended by the obvious surprise in her voice.

Rui's eyes fixed on the shelves lined with dozens of vinyl record covers.

"I used to."

Rui didn't say anymore, and Autumn decided not to push him further. She needed to focus on her role here. There was a formal dining room with nothing more than a distressed wood Trestle table and six cool gray-colored chairs. The living room had a desk, a leather chair on casters, and a half-empty bookcase. Okay, Houston we have a problem. Rui had converted the space into an office for himself, but everything for the office remained in the breakfast nook.

"Where will I sleep?" She imagined herself in Rui's arms, snuggled into his warmth. She gazed up at the angles of his face from beneath her lashes. He looked so sturdy, yet the state of the house revealed something about his in-flux state. Or maybe he wanted the old things to remain untouched, while his current life overshadowed the past. With quick steps he led her up a flight of stairs. There was a loft that overlooked the first floor. A door stood ajar revealing a full bath with a yellow ducky shower curtain. She peaked inside and saw a door she hadn't appreciated from the loft view. A nice-size bedroom with camel colored wood furniture adjoined the bathroom. With the added space of the loft, this floor was larger than the studio apartment she'd been kicked out of.

"This is beautiful, Rui." It was such a large space for one man and a little girl. She wondered if Rui had envisioned a big family when he purchased this house?

He squeezed her hand. "Simone and I use the rooms downstairs, but I want you to see all the rooms, so you can decide. There's two more bedrooms on this floor, but they share a bath."

"This way," Rui remarked, leading her down the staircase to a hallway nestled across from his office in a hidden alcove. They passed a small bath, and she stopped to peak inside. The room, painted a country blue, held a white pedestal sink, an American Standard commode, and an oversized tiled shower.

There were two doors, both of them closed. The first door they reached held an Asian-style fan made of blue silk hanging from pink laundry pins. The calligraphy script read, "Keep Out, Mei lives here."

Autumn had all but forgotten her new employment included her serving as guardian for a kid that probably needed a weekly therapy appointment with a priest, pastor, and a psychologist.

"Who's Mei?"

Rui grinned. "Mei is Simone's middle name. It means beautiful flower in Chinese. She's staked her claim as you can see."

What she saw was their interlocked fingers. Rui still held her hand. Autumn focused on the feel of his skin next to hers. She expected his hands to be smooth, but the pads of his fingers were rough like he worked with his hands.

Rui didn't bother to open the door to Simone's room. Instead they moved deeper down the hall. He twisted the knob and pushed the door open. On the back wall, three white lacquer frames depicted water cranes along a riverbank in soft brush-painted ink. Autumn was instantly in heaven. The room was large with an arched entryway to the ensuite bathroom that overlooked a private garden surrounded by an eight-foot privacy fence. Her heart rate beat a rapid staccato. She'd never stayed in a room this nice, not even as an adult.

Rui chuckled. "I assume by the way you're squeezing my hand that you've made your choice?"

"Oh," she winced. "Sorry."

Releasing Rui's hand, she stepped further into the space. Literally, she wanted to spin in a circle, break dance, and kick up her heels. She said a silent prayer of thanks that Simone Conners had jumped behind the wheel of Putter this morning.

She stopped at the bed, running her fingers over the soft quilt. Autumn studied the small details in the room: the ruffle drapes, the braided rug behind her feet, the paperback book next to the crystal lamp. This room was decorated by and for a woman. She felt a pang in her chest. Though Rui hadn't mentioned it, another woman was very much a part of his life.

"You like it?" he whispered, his deep voice in her ear.

She could feel the heat from his body caressing her back. Grabbing hold of her arms, she squeezed, quelling the urge to lean into him. How would it feel to lie in this bed with him beside her? Would the heat of him scorch the way she imagined? The air seemed to warm at the thought.

Rui's hands settled on her shoulders and she jumped.

"I'm sorry. I didn't mean to startle you."

His breath touched the side of her face. She knew she needed to step away, but she stayed planted.

Slowly, she placed on hand over his. "You don't scare me."

Though barely perceptible, she let her body sag into his. Neither of them moved, initially, but then he stiffened—every part of him.

Before she could talk herself out of it, she turned toward him. She slid her arms around his lean hips. Burying her face in his chest, she brushed her lips against the scattering of fine hair covering his chest. She thought she heard him suck in a breath, but she was lost in his scent. Clean, like the crisp pages of a leather-bound book, and rich musk like a man should be.

"Thank you, Rui," she said on a breathy whisper.

She expected him to push her away, but she sighed in relief when his arms firmed around her. A wave of sensual heat warred with the impropriety of her actions. The man was paying her.

"A-Autumn," he began. "I don't expect, that is, you don't have to give me...," he trailed off.

"I know," she said, releasing him. The second she stepped away, everything in her rebelled. Clinging to him had been the most comfort she'd felt in years. Already she missed being in his arms. But, she couldn't afford to jeopardize her position in this house. "I'm sorry," she managed to say. Sorry hadn't crossed her mind. She wanted to run her hands through his dark locks, cover his mouth with hers. Moan his name as-

"Autumn," he rasped. "I should grab your bags."

What was she doing? Was she really forcing herself on this man who'd helped her? Yes, she'd noticed him. Yes, there was attraction, but once again, she was making it easy. Her gaze snapped up to meet his. She'd gotten lost in the fantasy of what else she wanted from Rui Conners.

He cleared his throat. "After I unload, you stay here. Set up your room. I'll be back with Simone."

Face tight, he walked out of the room. Autumn had messed up. She wondered if he'd ever give her the chance to touch him again.

RUI slammed his hand on the steering wheel. Why the heck had he stopped Autumn from touching him? It had been years since a woman had shown him any tenderness, to include his interludes with Kirsten. He thought about how Autumn's mouth had softened at his invasion. The feel of her leaning on him, resting her head on his chest, renewed a sense of masculine pride he hadn't felt in ages. God, the woman had a sexy-as-sin way of showing her gratitude. Shoot, would she have offered those sweet berry lips if he'd been able to fix her piece of crap car?

Miller Road came into view, and Rui dropped his speed way below the limit to make the right turn. Owen's first wife, Caitlyn, God rest her soul, had been struck by a car on this very street. Though Owen kept up a good front for his son,

Cai, the townsfolk knew he blamed himself for his wife's death. Like Rui, he felt responsible for losing the woman entrusted to him. Thank heaven, Ivy had given him a new lease on love. Rui's heart thudded in his chest. Moving Autumn into his home had been the right decision but starting a relationship with a woman trying to get a lift-off on her dreams might be more risk than he needed. But, could Autumn be his second chance at forever?

In no time at all, Rui arrived at Endurance Elementary. A line of mini-vans, luxury and standard, formed a single-file line in front of the curb. His cellphone vibrated in his pocket. Before he could answer, the loud and clear sound of the bell rang signaling the end of the school day. The line started to move, so Rui let the call go to voicemail.

Rui expected to find Simone to be the first kid waiting for the security gate to be unlocked. With the school shootings happening in other parts of the country, the local school board had installed six-foot fencing with electronic locks surrounding the three school campuses in Endurance.

As he approached the orange-vested safety monitor, Rui lowered his window. The sound of his daughter's voice carried beyond his line of sight.

"Eight-year-olds don't need escorts."

He grinned. Simone was giving someone the riot act. He loved his daughter's spunk. She reminded him so much of Kirsten. The first night he'd met his former wife, she been wearing a chip on her shoulder as big as her voice. He'd sat through both sets as she and her band belted out jazzy and funk edified tunes until close to midnight. Her long body with its barely there curves had mesmerized him. The serpentine-like quality of her voice wound a hypnotic spell around him as he watched her sway to the rhythm. Kirsten was exquisite and full of laughter. After her last set, she'd surprised him by agreeing to a dance. At twenty-one, he'd been a young man with limited experience. Kirsten had shown him things he never imagined possible between two people. After that, no matter where or for how long she traveled, he'd waited, ever faithful, until she returned. That's how their relationship had worked. Rui had been Mr. Loyal and Steady while his exotic ebony beauty whisked herself away on one impulsive adventure followed by another.

Before Kirsten, his life had been a studious and isolated existence. His parents had disliked Kirsten on sight. They thought her too worldly for their boy genius. It was exactly the reason Rui was drawn to Kirsten. With her, he was welcomed into a world full of sound, color, and laughter. Everyday with his wife had been a party, even when Simone was born, he'd loved every sleepless night, every spilled jar of food, every unidentifiable stain on the carpet. But, motherhood had changed Kirsten. She missed the lights, the audience, and the adoration. Though she had a daughter and husband who adored her, she needed the pulse of the crowd. So, when she mentioned a European tour, he encouraged her. Wanted to see the spark in her eyes again, not realizing with her gone, he would lose his.

The car door opened. "I want pizza tonight," Simone ordered, closing the door.

"Hello to you, too."

She looked over at him. "Why do I have play nice with her, Daddy?"

He rubbed his face in frustration. They'd had this conversation more than once. "Being courteous costs you nothing. You should be polite to others."

She shrugged. "I'll think about it."

On the road, he passed the road leading to home and the town center. She looked up from her cell phone. "Pizza."

"No."

Her head snapped in his direction.

"You said no," she paused. Several seconds ticked by before she asked, "You dying?"

Had it been that long since he'd denied his only child?

Glancing at her, he frowned. "Not nice."

She dropped the phone into her lap. The Jeggings had been a birthday gift from her mother two years past. Simone had struggled to hide her tears when Kirsten had forgotten to mail her gift this year. Rui had tried to make things better, buying Simone a six-hundred-dollar smart phone. It had worked, but she'd stopped asking about her mom coming home after that.

"So, you're not dying?"

Face tight, he took one of the narrow roads leading to the mountain trails.

"No. Enough about death. You and I need to talk about this morning."

She dropped her head. "What about it?" Little shoulders hunched over. "That car was a piece of crap. Stealing it was a favor."

Rui had to hide his laugh. Simone was correct. If something had happened, the insurance carrier would probably write the car off of as a total loss and stroke Autumn a check."

"It was wrong."

Simone picked up the phone, twisting the blasted attention-sucker in hands that used to curl around his in fascination. She'd been such an inquisitive baby. With big brown eyes flitting around the room, she observed everything around her baby domain. Rui had changed her mobiles every week. He would read her bedtimes stories every night to keep her mind engaged. She seemed to light up the more he exposed her to environmental differences. Kirsten had called him insufferable. No, he had loved being a husband and a father. He still wanted that life.

Reaching across the console, he lifted her chin. A flash of shame colored her cheeks.

"Sorry," she mumbled.

"You owe Miss Autumn an apology, too."

After a quick nod, she said. "I will when I see her again."

This was the moment he'd been leading up to. "You're in luck."

She stopped fumbling with the phone. "How?"

"I know where she is?"

"Where?"

He started the car.

"At home waiting for you." Adrenaline spiked in his system at the thought of Autumn at home waiting on them. "She's your nanny. Starting today." He knew it was wrong, the thrill pumping through his veins.

"I don't need a babysitter."

"Watch it, Simone. Your tone is going to get you grounded." He could tell by the abrupt paleness of her skin that she understood he meant to deliver on his promise.

"She won't stay."

There was a time when a flippant response would never fall from Simone's lips. Rui had been her best friend, and then he wasn't. Now, she needed something he couldn't supply. Maybe, he and Autumn could find the answer...together. She was his daughter's nanny, not his. But for some reason, he had a hard time denying that a part of her was there for him, too.

CHAPTER FIVE

Had Autumn actually thrown herself into her boss's arms and kissed his chest? Yes. She wondered how far she would have pushed him if he hadn't stopped her. When he returned home, should she act as if the kiss never happened? Technically, did lips to torso count? Maybe, kissing a man's chest was equivalent to kissing a woman's hand. Courteous. Nah, she'd have to do something to make amends. An idea struck, to make up for her slip in decorum. With both Rui and Simone out of the house, she could get a lot accomplished.

Autumn made quick work of putting away her clothes and setting up her toiletries. She tackled the kitchen first. Rooting around in the pantry, she found a large plastic bag. The empty food boxes were the first to go. Next, she folded the clothes, and put the canned goods in the pantry. Then she transferred the books to Rui's office. It took her a minute to figure out his shelving system. After she cleared the bulk items off the tables, she found the offensive smelling gray, green, and brown chicken nuggets in a balled up fast food bag. Wrinkling her nose, she grabbed the putrid stench with gloved hands and deposited it in the trash can outside the back door. The gush of fresh air helped to clear her nostrils and her head. She decided to leave the door open and lift the window over the sink.

With the stench gone, the table and counter top cleared, she started looking through the cabinets orienting herself to the pots, pans, and utensils. For a man, Rui had a well-stocked kitchen and pantry. Finding the ingredients for a vegetable soup, she pulled a pot from behind the stove top and set the water to boil. The house was too quiet.

With the touch of a button, she streamed a soulful rhythm and blues number from Aria Arie's Lover Mine through the fragrant space. By the time Rui arrived home with Simone, she was singing along with the music and setting the oven timer.

She spun to find a slack-jawed Rui and a wide-eyed Simone staring at her.

"Wow," Simone said, scowling. "It smells weird in here."

Autumn smirked. "It's called fresh air."

Rui didn't move. Actually, he stared at the iPhone pumping the house full of bass and frowned. He examined the cleared table, the folded clothes, and then her.

Autumn ducked her head and turned off the music. She was unsure how he'd respond to her taking the liberty to start organizing his house. What had gotten into her? Never would she walk into someone else's house and take it upon herself to start cleaning and tossing out stuff she deemed trash. She opened her mouth to apologize.

"I love it," he said before she could speak. "Do I smell dinner?"

She nodded and smiled. He wasn't upset. "Yes. I used some of the fresh vegetables."

"Great," he said stepping in the house. "How long before food is on the table?"

Simone scowled at her. "I want pizza."

Autumn felt her smile slip. What kid chose pizza over a home-cooked meal? All of them. Her aunt rarely had the money to splurge on ready-made food. The few field trips they had been able to afford, Autumn had felt no shame asking for a second helping of fries, pizza, burgers, or cake. Sadness washed over her, but Rui's easy smile at such a small gesture overtook her.

"You have about ten minutes. The rolls are almost ready."

He approached, and then brushed his shoulder against hers. A tingle skirted up her arm. Had he deliberately touched her? Maybe, he felt the same pull that she did.

"I have a few emails to answer."

"Yeah, me too," Simone said, dropping her backpack by the door.

"Not so fast, young lady." Autumn might as well lay down the ground rules now. "Your backpack goes with you to your room."

"Dad," she whined. "She's being mean to me."

Rui crossed muscled arms over his chest. "I think she's being nice considering you haven't apologized."

So, he had addressed this morning with his daughter. Autumn's respect for him grew in that moment. Recalling the anger she felt at the police station, she was happy to see she'd been wrong about Rui. His justice, though not swift, was administered.

"Go on now. Look her in the eye and apologize."

Autumn waited, hoping her discomfort didn't show.

"Sorry," Simone muttered.

Autumn nodded in acceptance. "Apology accepted. Thank you."

With apologies made and accepted, dinner was a quiet affair. Both Rui and Simone ate heartily. Inwardly, Autumn beamed that she'd provided for her temporary family. She knew it was hokey, but they belonged to each other for now, so she'd enjoy being included.

After dinner, Rui volunteered to clean up the kitchen, while Simone disappeared behind her bedroom door.

Autumn peered in the child's direction.

"Don't worry. I usually have her choose her school clothes before bed."

At eight, Simone should have some role in readying her clothes for the next day.

Rui must have followed her train of thought. "She'd wear the same pair of leggings everyday if she could."

Autumn had noticed the pant legs were creeping up Simone's rail thin legs.

"I remember doing the same at that age." More because her aunt didn't put much in the budget from replacing Autumn's clothes each school year.

"I can start helping her with her wardrobe," she offered.

Rui paused in his ministrations with the dishes. "That would be alright."

Was he implying some activities were off limits?

"Maybe you should define my duties here."

"You can do what you want."

Like kiss the boss when she wanted?

She laughed. "Somehow, I don't think that's how employment works."

Rui sighed. "You're right. How about you go check on Simone while I finish up here? We'll talk afterwards."

She nodded and padded away, confused by Rui's unease with giving her instructions. No man would unleash a complete stranger on his child without some parameters. What was going through his head? Maybe, her actions had scrambled his brain, too.

Autumn knocked on Simone's bedroom door. When she twisted the knob, the door slid opened. With Simone's short comments over dinner, she half expected the door to be locked.

Unlike the entertaining spaces, Simone's four poster bed was free of clutter. A mounted chalk board over the bed proclaimed, Princess Simone's throne in bold pink letters. Two rows of LED lights had been used to form the shape of a princess-worthy ball gown on the wall next to the attached bathroom. It was an ingenious way to install a nightlight for a little girl that would surely object to such a practical utility. Around the upper left bed post hung a crown of chrome plastic with hot pink plastic jewels, while white tulle hung in wavy swatches surrounding the bed. In the corner, a small white-washed desk held framed photos of Simone from birth to current day, and a small assortment of stuffed animals. The love poured into creating this storybook world pulled at her heart strings. Simone's mother had outdone herself. It made Autumn want to ask after the woman who so obviously adored her daughter. This is how every little girl should be treasured.

"What are you looking at?" Simone snapped.

The enchantment bubble burst. "Your father asked me to choose your clothes for in the morning."

"Already done. You can leave."

The fact that Simone dismissed her while her fingers flew across her smartphone keyboard, well...it smarted.

Autumn approached the bed. She would not be run off by an eight-year-old tyrant. "Look, Simone. I would like us to be friends."

Legs folded under her butt Indian-style, Simone uncoiled her limbs. "Back up, lady. I don't know you like that."

Realizing this was a fight for dominance, Autumn further encroached by sitting on the edge of the bed. "My being here is important to your father. He cares about you, so let's play nice together." She smiled trying to coax the child to her side. "What do you say, friends?" Autumn extended her hand in a peace offering.

The little miscreant looked at her hand, bare of jewelry and nail color, like she had stuck it up her nose in front of the whole school.

"Sorry, lady. I get to choose my friends."

At the rejection, Autumn snatched her hand back from the venomous words. The response was irrational, but after years of having her olive branch trampled on, she was less than willing to offer twice in one night. Tomorrow, she told herself would be better.

Stiffening her chin, she said, "Fine." She came to her feet. "It this your closet?" Autumn pointed to the only closed door in the room.

"Yeah, why?" Simone scrambled from the bed, socked feet hitting the floor with a muffled thud.

"Let's see your clothes for tomorrow."

"I can dress myself," Simone said in a confident tone. The kid didn't back down. Autumn admired her spunk. Then she physically moved her out of the way.

"Hey," the girl protested. "Put me down."

"Sure thing."

On the closet handle, a pink t-shirt with a rainbow unicorn hung in front of a pair of pink denim jeans. Cute pairing, but she didn't see any shoes.

"Which shoes?" Autumn asked without looking behind her.

"Haven't decided."

There was a curious note in Simone's tone, so Autumn took a chance. "Sandals or a pair of Uggs might work."

A little body darted beneath her arm and entered the well-organized space.

"I have two pairs. Tan with fur and black with white inside.

Autumn smiled to herself. Gotcha. She felt the fine web of a friendship begin.

"Black matches everything, but tan makes a fashion statement."

Simone wrinkled her nose. "Kids don't make statements."

"Of course they do." She counted off on her fingers. "In magazine ads, television commercials, and on the internet."

"So, you, uh, are an adult, right?"

Autumn sucked in a long pull of air sure that she'd addressed this topic to the fullest extent.

"Simone," she warned.

"Okay," she huffed. "It's just that," she hesitated. "There's a mommy-daughter tea at school."

"Yeah," Autumn said, eager to help.

"Well, I don't know nothing about tea. My teacher said we should practice dancing too. My, my mom probably can't come with me."

Simone stopped talking. Autumn frowned, and then waited, hoping the kid would break the silence. The little girl's taut shoulders spoke volumes. This conversation was hard for both of them. Without having any details, she knew the absence of Simone's mother had left deep wounds.

Autumn moved closer. "I can help you. We can try different teas," she said adding more enthusiasm than warranted to her voice. "We'll need music, but you can practice your dance steps with me."

With a raised brow, Simone gave Autumn a twisted frown.

Okay, she was a poor replacement for a mother, but this could work. "Hey," she chided. "Only if you want to or until your mom comes."

With a furrowed brow, her new charge considered the offer, and then gave it a nod of approval.

"Great. We can start tomorrow after I speak with your teacher."

"My dad said my mom was on television once."

On impulse, Autumn reached down and brushed a hand over Simone's reddish-brown locks.

"If she's half as pretty as you, I bet she was," she whispered. At the compliment, Simone's sharp comments took on a more rounded edge.

"She left us. My mom."

It was said with such bluntness, Autumn stood stunned for a second.

"You don't ever leave people you love, even if you're apart," Autumn said. Did she really believe those words? If that was the case, she was doomed. Autumn thought back to her bedroom. Rui's house was another woman's shrine. It didn't matter. She was here to help Simone. Rui's love life didn't involve her.

"Let me put an app on your phone to help you learn the different types of tea leaves. And," she beamed remembering a little jewel she'd found while cleaning the kitchen, "there's a Terra Cotta tea set tucked away in the pantry. I'll ask your dad can we use it."

Simone didn't share her enthusiasm, but she handed over the phone. Autumn took it as a positive sign.

Later, when she entered the family room, she found Rui placing the last of the dishes in the cupboard, still dressed in his clothes from earlier.

"What are you doing?" She would've taken care of tidying the kitchen. Autumn believed in honoring her commitments. Housekeeping, including the kitchen cleanup was a part of her job.

"Helping out," he said, brow raised. "You look surprised."

She told him the truth. "A little. I guess I'm used to doing everything myself."

Depending on folks to help her hadn't been an option...until now. Endurance had some drawbacks, but the way people pitched in to help anyone in need made this town special. Owen let her eat meals at the bar when her cash ran low. Ivy, his wife, she considered a best friend and confidant. Now, Rui had given her a safe place to lay her head and a job. She shouldn't ask for more, but...

"Can Simone and I use that Terra Cotta server for the mother-daughter tea?"

She stopped under the arched entryway. This was probably a safe distance. She hoped.

"Sure," he replied without hesitation.

Maybe the tea set wasn't a part of the shrine. Though it was a bit forward, she asked the question that had bugged her from the moment he gave her a tour of the house. "Are you married or something?"

"I was." His lips quirked at the corners, like he wasn't sure he spoke the truth. "Little late to ask considering what happened this afternoon."

"What did happen?" She knew what her intentions were. Less than honorable, but what had he been thinking not to push her away?

"We both had a challenging day," was his only comment.

"So, you helped me out of pity?"

He pushed away from the counter. When he stood before her, she swallowed her fear, and looked up into his fathomless eyes.

"There's nothing pitiful about you, Autumn Raine."

If he only knew. As if he'd read her mind, he challenged, "Don't go digging in the past to prove me a liar."

"Never," she whispered. He was one of the most honest men she'd met. The way he'd admitted to not knowing a thing about cars had shocked her. There was no defensive bravado in his tone, just truth.

"Rui," she swallowed. "I'm sorry about the kiss. I had no right."

He placed a finger over her mouth. The gesture was so intimate; his touch perfection. Confident that he would welcome her touch, Autumn raised up on her toes and pressed her lips to his. His response was immediate. He moved his lips with a slow ease that communicated warmth and acceptance.

Gosh, he tasted amazing. Any apprehension she felt, melted away. Autumn lifted her arms, draping them around his neck, pulling him closer. When he slid his arm up her back, encircled her waist, and tugged her into his hard body, she moaned. She could go on like this forever.

"Do you want to have sex?"

Forever came to an abrupt halt. She took a step back to stare at the man she just kissed.

"Now?" she questioned, disbelief lending a high pitch to her voice.

"Yes."

"No, Rui." Her rejection seemed to dull some of the hunger burning in his eyes. What a mess. "Sorry," she said sucking her lip between her teeth. "Considering I'm the one who keeps touching you, I'm sure it's me who's sending mixed signals."

"Never apologize for wanting to touch me. I tend to rush forward when I'm interested in a woman."

It wasn't exactly an invitation for a repeat performance, but it was an admission. Obviously, Rui had interest in forging a new relationship, so why did the house look like he was committed to the old one? Just how connected was Rui to the invisible woman she felt in every room, even standing between them.

It had been a long time since any man sparked this intense need in her. She found herself reluctant to walk away without making an effort. Even if an affair with Rui Conners ended in heartbreak, she'd test her luck. She couldn't sink any lower than she already was. So, with a shaky hand, but a steady voice, she asked the question that would change everything. To win the bonus round, please let him answer the jeopardy question correctly.

"Where's Simone's mother?" She felt his body tense. That couldn't be good.

EVERYTHING inside Rui stilled at Autumn's question. There was something inherently wrong talking about Kirsten to another woman. Especially while standing in the home he'd purchased for his then-wife.

He heard the chill in his voice but felt helpless to quell the sharp edge. "She's not a problem."

Why did she have to ask questions? Coming home to a semi-clean house and a fresh cooked meal had been a fantasy come true. Kirsten could barely cook up an appetite. His ex-wife had been obsessed with her weight, her hair, her clothes, and her make-up. The list was never ending. To see Autumn with natural hair, her face and nails bare of anything artificial was refreshing. She was so different from Kirsten. The pull of attraction between them intrigued him.

Autumn frowned. "I see," she said, and moved further away from him. He felt the muscles in his forearm tense, ready to grab her if she ran. The reaction was unnatural. Never in his life, had he restrained a woman against her will. But, he didn't want Autumn to run away from him. No, quite the opposite. He wanted this woman to run into his arms, time and time again.

He gestured toward the couch in the other room. "Let's sit down."

"I'll stand." She licked her lips and he thought he heard an answering rumble from his own throat.

"What do you mean when you say she's not a problem?"

He didn't want to talk about Kirsten. Not now, not ever. Autumn was good and pure. He didn't want to taint her with his ugliness. But, where the air between them was once charged with pulsing energy, a coolness had taken hold. Autumn was withdrawing, and Rui needed the warmth he sensed in her. He'd give her something to ease her mind, but he'd keep more than he'd give away.

"We're divorced. She lives in Germany. Has for the last three years."

Why his comment seemed to add to the unexpected wall between them he didn't know, but again, he never did understand the female mind. Women claimed to want the security of a husband and home, but then they discarded both without looking back. Fickle creatures, all of them.

"So, it's over?"

He released a grunt in frustration. Isn't that what he just said?

"Yes, for my part."

"And, hers?"

He smiled remembering the soulful singer he'd met all those years ago. "Can't speak for her but...yeah, I guess."

"You sound unsure."

He rubbed his goatee, letting the repetitive motion tamp down his pent-up frustration. "Can't speak for Kirsten. Never could."

"I...I mean, you sound unsure about you."

He flinched as if she'd slapped him. His temper flared, but he managed to hold on to the reins.

"I'm an educated man, Miss Raine. I know when to call it quits."

"So, you ended the marriage?"

Heck no. He would have never left his wife.

"A man doesn't walk away from his responsibilities," he ground out.

He hadn't meant to sound so harsh. It had been years since anyone had asked after his wife. Autumn's questions unsettled him. Why were they even having this discussion? Because he'd allowed her to kiss him. Truth be told, he wanted her to do a lot more, before he took control.

She nodded. "I see," she whispered.

What the hell could she possibly see, when he was damn near blinded with the need to take her into his arms?

"Autumn."

"Good night, Professor Conners. I'll see you in the morning."

She turned and walked away.

Shoot, he'd done it again. Another woman in his life had left him standing...alone.

CHAPTER SIX

Autumn spent the night tossing and turning about her new boss. But, she had made a decision. Rui Conners was off-limits to her. Autumn refused to get involved with another man who was emotionally unavailable. She believed him when he'd told her about his wife, but there was more there...hidden. Well, Rui could keep his hard body and secrets to himself. She had a job to do, and a race to win.

With the alarm clock set for four in the morning, Autumn was out of bed before the first glow of morning. She ran her ten miles before Simone or Rui had stirred. She'd finished the run with forty-five seconds to spare, a new training record. The new route had invigorated her. What surprised her was Simone and Rui had to be roused from sleep. Because she liked to eat something after a full run, she had breakfast ready when her new employer and her ward appeared in the kitchen. Rui had tried to engage her in conversation. She stuck to the morning pleasantries, not wanting to give the remote impression that what happened yesterday would happen again.

The drive to the Endurance elementary was a quiet one.

"Autumn, why don't you come in and meet Ms. Springfield. I'll add your name to the list of authorized persons to pickup and drop-off Simone at school."

With her car still in the lot at Tommy's Park, Autumn would be dependent on Rui for transportation for a while. Rui had the car waiting for her and Simone by the time she prepped Simone's lunch.

"Do I have to take this lunch?"

"Well," Rui began.

"Yes," Autumn looked down at the child walking between the two of them. "Did you even look in the bag?"

"No, but I won't like it," Simone said with a smirk on her face. Okay, the truce declared over the fashion last night had obviously ended.

"Try it, and then we'll talk after school."

Simon looked to Rui. "Dad, do I have to?"

Autumn waited to see if he would support her. Not that she would walk away from the job, but it would be much easier to stop fantasizing about him if he was a spineless jellyfish.

"You heard Autumn."

Though her face remained unchanged, Autumn was beaming on the inside.

"Fine, but I won't eat it."

Autumn had worked in an elementary school as a teacher's aide in the San Diego County Unified school district. What they served for school lunch, students should band together and write their congressman. The bag held two servings of fresh fruit, nuts, an organic whole yogurt and a note wishing Simone a great day.

"Simone, walk Autumn to your class while I handle the paperwork in the front office."

A huff came a second before a flat. "Okay."

Ms. Springfield, Simone's third grade teacher, was a slender-face woman with huge glasses and chestnut brown hair cut in a severe bob. Her slender body was draped in a sac-like brown frock straight out of Uncle Fester's wardrobe. Though Autumn appreciated the symmetry in Ms. Springfield's features, the woman was a walking eye sore. It was almost painful to look at the her.

"Hello, I'm Autumn," she introduced herself.

Wow, Autumn hoped it was a disguise because without the bad hair and worse clothes, Kelby Springfield was a looker.

"Go on to your seat, Simone," the woman said while accepting her hand.

"Autumn," she repeated, eyes darting between her and Simone, probably trying to gage the connection. "So," she drug out the word. "You'll be ensuring Simone gets to class? I haven't seen you before. Are you new in Endurance?"

"Eight months give or take a week," Autumn supplied, sure the educator was asking more for herself than out of concern for Simone's educational well-being.

"How does your family like small town living?"

Yep, definitely trying to figure out the connection.

"Simone, is that your mommy?" a boy, with pale skin, and dark eyes teased. There were snickers from the other kids. Autumn immediately felt outrage. How dare these kids target her because of her mother's actions.

In what Autumn was discovering to be true Simone fashion, the little girl rounded on her would-be taunter. "Shut up and mind your business, Boy Moana."

All the laughter halted. Whoa. Simone Conners commanded mad respect. In some ways, Autumn wished she had the same fearless gene. Maybe, she wouldn't have spent so many recess sessions alone and in tears.

Good for Simone for defending her, but aloud she said, "Simone, play nice."

Taking her seat at the center desk, Simone plopped down her backpack. "I did."

Autumn hid her smile. The boy was lucky two adults were in the room to keep him safe.

"I'll be here after school," Autumn supplied, wanting the other kids to know Simone had someone in her corner. Autumn remembered how it felt to be teased, knowing it would only get worse after the school bell rung.

"Whatever," Simone said.

When Autumn turned to leave. Ms. Springfield said, "I hope to see you at the mother-daughter tea in a few weeks. All the girls have been practicing their manners and dance steps."

Autumn paused. Could this have anything to do with Simone skipping school? Just then she heard a commotion erupting in the class.

"Wait." Simone came running forward. "Can you mail this letter for me."

Autumn studied the name written in neat bold letters, Kirsten Conners. So, the kid kept in contact with her mom. Nice to know she had some semblance of a relationship with her other parent. Autumn hadn't heard from her mother in years. Not that she and her aunt were close, but she would have told her if her mother had contacted her seeking Autumn out.

"Your mom?"

"Yeah," Simone said, her voice uncharacteristically soft.

Autumn, reached for her, then thought better of it with all the onlookers. "I'll take care of it."

Simone gave her the first genuine smile. "Thanks, Autumn."

"You're welcome," she said, but Simone was gone. To Ms. Springfield she said, "That's Simone's decision.

The teacher nodded in understanding. "Yes," she sighed. "But, maybe you could help her with her dance steps," she suggested, her voice tentative. "Have my hands full with the play list."

Now, this was something Autumn could help with. After getting an explanation about the mother-daughter tea, Autumn volunteered to compile a playlist for the event. She thought it might help to associate each choreographed routine to a specific song. Ms. Springfield, whose first name was Kelby, eagerly accepted. Together, they devised a plan to download a playlist the girls could take home and share with their parents. It would help everything flow smoothly on event day.

Back in the car, Autumn updated Rui of the tea and her plan to help. He maneuvered the car out onto the road.

"Well now, you just jump right in with both feet, don't you? How did you sleep last night?"

"Fine," she lied. He didn't need to know that thoughts of him waylaid her dreams causing a fitful night.

"You want to tell me why you're being short."

"I'm not," she replied, keeping her eyes straight ahead.

"Can you drop me by No Limit?" She would ask Owen to help with her car until payday.

"I can. Why?"

She gave him an incredulous look. "Because Owen will help me with the car tow."

He stared at her as if she'd just pooped in his favorite running shoes. "I took care of it. Raymond will deliver it to the house in a few days when the repairs are completed."

She was momentarily speechless. "When?"

"Yesterday after I picked up Simone."

So, he'd taken care of her car before their stilted conservation last night.

She managed a stiff, "Thank you."

"You're welcome. Now, answer my question."

"Which is?"

"Why the cold shoulder this morning?"

There was no denying the chill that had settled after yesterday's hot and heavy kissing, but Autumn had to protect her heart. She'd been burned by too many people who were supposed to care about her. She didn't want to add Rui to the list.

They waited at a stoplight.

"Look, Professor." He turned to face her with those exotic eyes. "I already apologized for overstepping my boundaries."

"I never said that."

She shook her head dismissing his objection. "I don't believe you're available to me."

"I didn't lie to you. I was married, now I'm divorced."

"Not intentionally. But, I've already had my run-in with a single man who was very much attached." Her first and only boyfriend had dragged her heart over the asphalt and she still had the road rash to prove it. Never again would she play second chair to another woman. "Not being married, doesn't make you available, it-,"

That's all she got out before Rui's lips were on hers. His kiss was warm, wet, and Autumn realized that she was all too willing. A blaring car horn signaled it was time for them to move forward. Even as she allowed him deeper inside, she thought about running...to him...or away, she wasn't sure, anymore.

RUI gritted his teeth as he and Autumn walked into No Limit Bar & Grille. Ivy and Owen were behind the bar. The usual morning crowd, Hank Stewart and Luke Cole, both building maintenance guys at the university occupied stools along the counter. The smell of fresh brewed coffee and buttermilk pancakes hit Rui's nostrils, and his mouth watered. Breakfast with Autumn was definitely on the menu.

Both Hank and Luke spun on their stools, studying them.

"Morning, Professor," Hank said, shooting a questioning look to Autumn. "You okay, honey?"

Rui grimaced. Honey. Like Rui, Hank had solo parenting duties to a ten-year-old fishing addict by the name of Elliott. The kid had a fishing reel glued to his little hand.

"We were worried about you," Luke chimed in.

Word had spread through town that Autumn had a change of address. Maybe, he and Autumn didn't have time for breakfast. Their kiss in the car had done little to change her mind. She was panting when they broke apart, her chest heaved, but her eyes remained resolute. Rui on the other hand, had to adjust his mind to them being together and his Dockers.

"I'm fine," Autumn reassured them all.

Neither of them was fine. She still thought he was hung up on his ex-wife. That would be stupid. And, Rui was not a stupid man. Last night he'd allowed two of Kirsten's calls to go to voicemail. Not in the mood for her games, he decided to deal with her messages after work, after he took care of the woman before him. Autumn had priority, whether she wanted it or not. Now, she wanted to spend time with Owen and Ivy, instead of him. He suspected a part of her still wanted to ask the other man for help. No way would Rui stand by while she accepted anything from another man. He would provide for her.

Ivy looked up from the ledgers spread out at the end of the bar. She smiled. "Good morning, you two."

With wild ringlets framing her salted vanilla skin, a tie-dye t-shirt, ripped jeans, and combat boots, Ivy Summers looked liked the rebel she was. She'd walked into town not too long ago and stolen the widower Owen's heart. The scowl on Owen's face had been as much a part of him as his arm or leg before Ivy came along. Now, the man laughed louder than a kid in an ice cream shop everyday.

Rui was happy for them both, but that didn't mean they could interfere where he and Autumn were concerned. He knew Autumn didn't want to be beholden to him. What adult woman would? But, there was something growing between them and he wouldn't allow her to derail their two trains connecting. Last night as he lay in bed, he thought about how a relationship with Autumn could be good for both of them. She needed someone to look after her, and he needed a woman that was all his.

From his bedroom window, he'd watched Autumn start her morning run up the hill leading away from the house. Her stride was sure, measured, and steady. Once she reached the top, she gained speed, and then disappeared from his sight. His heart rate increased, his pulse raced, and his body ached. He could be the man at her finish line. Rui could wait for her to come around, but first she needed to start moving in his direction, not away.

"I'm doing well, Ivy." Autumn's smile didn't quite reach her eyes.

"Hey, Ivy. Good to see you," Rui said giving her shoulder a squeeze. When Ivy arrived in town, she'd sought him out to the bar owner's dismay. Initially suspicious, Rui was prepared to wave off her advances. Nothing could have been farther from the truth. As a child, Ivy confessed she struggled with reading and comprehension. Too late in her formal education, it was discovered that she had dyslexia. Unfortunately, by the time of the discovery, her self-esteem had taken a major blow. Because of his academic background, Ivy had sought his help with education classes designed with her dyslexia in mind. Even though she hadn't asked him to, he'd monitored her progress from afar. He was glad to know she still attended weekly classes.

Right now, he was more concerned with what he saw on Autumn's face. The raw hurt reflected there bothered Rui. She'd been passionate last night, eager to touch him. He wanted that again. Somehow his explanation about his relationship with Kirsten had more than disappointed her; he'd hurt her. While she'd prepared Simone's lunch, she'd pretended business as usual, but she'd struggled to maintain the façade. Was the pretense for his benefit or hers? The short responses, the cold shoulder, and the reactions felt more extreme than the situation warranted. He made a mental note to ask her what the hell was going on?

Ivy frowned and approached Autumn. "I heard about what happened with your place."

Pulling out a chair from one of the four-seater tables in the dining area, Autumn collapsed into the cushioned seat.

Owen came around the bar, not stopping until he reached Autumn. "I drove out to your place last night after I heard the news. Perez is a royal nut tart for tossing your stuff out like that. Why didn't you call us?" Owen asked, taking the seat opposite Autumn.

At least six feet tall, with his thick blond hair and striking blue eyes, Owen Tate looked like a Norse god.

"Because I took care of her."

Everyone turned to looked at Rui. He'd heard about enough of Owen's alpha male machismo. Ivy and Cai were Owen's responsibility. Not Autumn.

He met the other man's eyes. That's right, Rui thought, mind your own business.

"Oh, I wasn't aware you and Autumn were close."

"We are," Rui snapped.

Ivy looked at Autumn. Pointing at Rui, she asked. "You down with OPP?"

What? "I know what that means. I'm not other people's property."

Laughing, Ivy snorted. "Not property, over protective professor."

"Owen," Autumn interjected. "Rui offered me a job as his daughter's nanny."

Owen kept his gaze fixed on Rui. "Is that so?"

"Yeah, it is," Rui offered, not liking what he saw in the other man's face.

"Where are you staying, Autumn?"

Endurance being a small noisy town, Owen knew the answer to his question before he asked.

She stammered a little before saying, "Ah, the job comes with room and board."

Owen narrowed his eyes, expression going hard. "You think that's a good idea?"

What the heck? Now, the bartender was trying to sabotage his relationship. Okay, Rui was a bit premature with the titles, but there was a pull between him and Autumn.

"Yes," he ground out. "We thought it the best option."

Ivy chimed in. "Well," she smiled, trying to cut through the peanut butter-thick tension between him and Owen. "You can always stay here."

Autumn looked from him to Owen, and then to Ivy. Was she considering moving out because what happened during their talk last night?

"Autumn has a place to stay for as long as she wants."

Owen crossed his arms over his chest. "Seems a bit much, Rui. Nannies come and go."

What was he supposed to say to that? Autumn was more than Simone's nanny and Owen damn well knew it.

"Look, I brought Autumn by so you both would know that she's fine."

Ivy chuckled. "Professor, I don't think I've ever seen you this animated. You've made your point."

"Which is?" he snapped.

"Watch it, Rui," Owen growled, coming to his feet.

Rui stepped up in Owen's face. "I could say the same."

Autumn stood. "Hey, hey," she sighed. "No chest-thumping allowed."

"Ah, Autumn, let them fight. At least wait till first blood," Hank chuckled.

Luke grinned. "Yeah, I was about to ask Ivy for popcorn and a beer."

Rui looked at her incredulously. "He started it."

"Me," Owen said, tone accusatory. "You're the one going all Conan the Barbarian. I took care of it-grunt. She's staying with me-grunt. Grunt."

Rui stared before he said, "I was wrong."

"About?" Owen questioned.

"About you being a changed man. You're still an ass."

Owen chuckled at that, and the women followed suit. "I can provide whatever Autumn needs."

"Never said you couldn't my friend. Just trying to help out, Rui."

"Listen," Autumn chimed in. "Before things get more freakily awkward."

"Too late," Ivy laughed.

"About me watching Cai," Autumn's voice dropped low.

Rui could hear the guilt lacing her words.

Ivy waved off Autumn's sadness. "Owen and I can manage with Cai. Besides, Rui's gig is full-time."

"Yeah," Autumn said. "Thanks for being understanding. I'll miss Cai."

"No worries," Ivy smiled. "Bring Simone by sometimes. She and Cai can veg out in the backyard or at Tommy's Park."

Autumn lit up. "That's a great idea."

Ivy beamed. "Yeah, I'm brilliant like that."

Owen grabbed his woman around the waist and kissed her lips. "So modest."

Ivy kissed him back, a playful, quick peck. "You have no idea."

These two were so right for one another, Rui thought. And, Owen was right. Rui was being hyper paranoid. Since Kirsten's departure, it bothered him that his wife had been unhappy with the life he'd offered. What happened between him and Kirsten was impacting his interactions with Autumn. Was he going overboard? Heck, yeah.

He liked Autumn and didn't want her attention to wander. Maybe he would have felt better if Kirsten had left him for another man, but no. His wife had left him for a faceless crowd. When his love had been matched against a studio audience, a smoke-filled club, and a life spent in hotel rooms, he'd lost the one person who'd promised to love and cherish him forever. This time he wouldn't put his trust in love. No, this time he'd come out of the gate, sprinting to win.

He extended a hand to Autumn. "You've reported in. They can see that you're safe."

Ivy slapped at his shoulder. "Lighten up, professor. We just want Autumn to know she has options." She gave a mock grimace. "We're not taking Autumn away. Grunt. Grunt. Grunt."

Now, they were mocking him.

Looking to Autumn, he said. "You ready to go?"

Too much time around friends made him feel like crap. Was he taking advantage of Autumn's circumstances? She must have guessed the direction of his thoughts because she slipped her hand into his. Rui breathed in a sigh of relief and tightened his grip. She had chosen to leave with him.

"Yeah, I'm ready."

As they headed up Saratoga Springs Road, he vowed he'd do everything in his power to ensure she never regretted choosing to stay with him.

WHY had Autumn refused the out Owen and Ivy had given her? They couldn't have been clearer that she had a place to lay her head if she wasn't open to Rui's interest anymore. Lifting her eyes, she glanced at Rui through her lashes. The man beside her was so confusing. He didn't want to be honest about his feelings, yet he broadcasted his desire for her at the first opportunity.

She needed to set some boundaries, but first, she needed some time to think. When they entered the house, Autumn had every intention of heading straight to her room. Rui had class this evening, so she'd have the house to herself after she got Simone off to bed.

When they entered the house, he grabbed her arm. Before she could put some space between them, he pulled her into an embrace.

"Look, Autumn. I'm sorry if I embarrassed you back there."

She relaxed into his arms, loving the feel of her hand against his body. "It's okay."

He blew out a harsh breath. "It's not, sweetheart."

"Rui," she started. If she didn't get it out she knew that if he touched her anymore intimately she'd lose the ability to speak.

"I want you to stay."

She looked up at him, letting sincerity shine through in her eyes. "Rui, I'm here."

He stroked her cheek, and she angled her head to increase the contact. No man had ever touched her with such reverence. Even without saying a word, she could feel the hesitancy in his touch, as if she might break if he pressed to hard.

"No, sweetheart, I need you to understand."

"What am I missing?"

"I liked you from the first time I saw you. You're beautiful, and funny...and smart. And...and when you smile at me it lights my whole world." Her breath hitched. A tremble vibrated through her body. "My daughter likes you."

Autumn raised a brow at that, not so sure Simone would agree. "You sure about that?"

"Yeah, I am," he said, trailing his large hands down her arms. Tingles spread down her spine until she felt lifted off the ground. "Give me a chance to make you happy, Autumn."

He wanted her, but what would happen after she gave him her body? Would she be on the street again? Only this time, instead of her stuff being broken, it would be her heart.

"What if we don't, what if I don't ..."

"Shh. Just say yes." A rye grin spread across his handsome face. "Let's try. There's something special between us, Autumn. Tell me you feel it too."

"I do, and I want to, but Rui...I need this job."

Those onyx eyes that she could fall in love with seemed to bore into hers.

"Autumn, the two are mutually exclusive."

"Meaning?" She understood the term, but she needed him to explain how he saw their relationship playing out.

"I'm six years older than you and a single father. Any woman I'm involved with has to build a healthy relationship with my daughter, too. If you don't want this, then tell me."

She swallowed, but he had to ask. "And if I don't want the same with you. What about my job?"

"Dang it, woman. Sleeping with me isn't a condition of your employment."

"But if we don't work out, Rui." She shook her head, knowing if their relationship went south, so would she. She'd have to return to Chula Vista, without any money, without a degree, with nothing.

"Then, we'll have to make sure that doesn't happen." He smiled.

He kissed her lips. "I'm willing to do my part."

Autumn studied her boss's face. The lines crossing his forehead were softer than the ones bracketing his mouth. Tension. Though their conversation was sedate in terms of language, the topic warranted a post-surgical narcotic.

"You're serious?"

"Of course. You're vulnerable, Autumn."

She bristled at the comment. She'd been taking care of herself just fine before he came along. And she would have managed, even with the eviction.

"Let me finish," he admonished.

She gave a stiff nod, not totally convinced she wanted to hear anymore.

"I don't want you to ever feel that I'm taking advantage of you living in my home."

"I don't."

And, I believe you, but," his voice dropped low and husky. "I want you. When I hold you in my arms, all I can think about is getting closer, Autumn," he hesitated. "Much closer."

"I want you, too."

He stroked both hands down her arms, until he reached her hands. Once there, he interlocked their fingers.

"I haven't been with another woman since my ex-wife."

She stilled at the revelation. Rui Conners chose her to end his celibacy? Whoa, talk about pressure.

"I'm not telling you this to add any pressure to your decision."

"Then why?" Was he ready to open up and tell her what he'd held back last night?

"Because, I know there'll be times when I mess this up, Autumn. Please, be patient."

Did this mean they had a future beyond physical intimacy? She wanted to ask but was scared he'd run for the closest hill and keep going. It probably had been longer since she'd had a sexual relationship. It was like guys could see her issues coming. In high school, none of the boys were interested in her. By the time she'd reached college, her one sexual encounter was more or less to see what all the fuss was about. Much of nothing, in her opinion. In end, she ended up sore, unsatisfied, and coated with what felt like warm coconut Jell-O. When the next guy suggested they hook up, she had no problem saying, no, but thanks for asking.

"You'll be patient with me, too?"

"Of course, sweetheart, but first I need something."

She turned her face up to regard him. "What?"

"I've been aching to kiss you again. Honestly, I can think of little else."

She came up on tiptoe. "By all means, let's put you out of your misery."

Autumn barely knew Rui. Sure, she'd seen him in the bar and on campus for the past eight months, but did that count when she was preparing to sleep in his bed one day soon?

All of a sudden one of his arms tightened around her waist, and she felt her feet leave the ground.

"What..."

He lifted her with such ease. The unexpected show of power excited her. How else might he use his strength to please her?

"Wrap your legs around my waist," he ordered.

Well now, this certainly sounded promising, but she wasn't ready to go all the way.

In long strides he made his way to the couch. When she tried to release him, he gripped her hips.

"Straddle me," he said dropping to the couch.

She did as he asked. The position brought the most intimate parts of them in close contact. A steady buzz began in her belly.

"You are full of surprises, professor."

He nipped at the delicate skin on her neck in reply.

"I like it when you call me, professor."

She nipped his lips, and he hissed. "You taste good," she paused. "Professor."

She leaned forward. With her tongue she brushed across his lips. A slow smile spread across his face.

"Do that again for your professor."

Ah well now, she liked the sound of that. She knew it was all a part of the game, but she could pretend that this generous man belonged her. They didn't have much time together before Simone had to be picked up from school. He wanted her. And, God help her, Autumn wanted him.

She grinned and repeated her previous trek. Moistening her lips first, she touched her mouth to his before using her tongue. This time, he caught her between his teeth, sucking her tongue into his mouth. Sugar plum fairy, it felt amazing. How had she existed so long without this man? Now that she'd had a sample, there was no way she could deny herself any longer.

"Mmm," she moaned.

"Dang, woman," he growled. "You're the smoothest melody."

Her. Autumn felt like she was floating on a cloud. Her whole body felt as if she might ignite. As he deepened the kiss, Rui's lids had dipped to half-mast. She didn't want to miss a moment, but all too soon her eyes closed, and she started to fly.

Deftly, she extricated her shirt ends from her pants. The warmth of his hands on her waist, and then her exposed flesh, had her heart racing. Her insides flooded in a pool of warmth. The sensation was so foreign, the sensual sounds tumbling from her mouth surprised her. She felt him everywhere.

"More, Rui," she whispered.

The cool air brushed across her skin. Damn, he was good. When had he removed her shirt?

"Patience, sweetheart," he mumbled between kisses.

Kisses that he trailed down her neck and lower. When he took one of her peaks in his mouth, she cried out in pleasure.

'Yes," she hissed. "Like that."

She'd heard he was a master orator in the classroom. The way he worked her over with a twisted array of strokes, sucks, and tugs gave her the highest expectations that he would put those skills to use in the bedroom.

"I want you in my bed," he mumbled, before giving her other rounded globe the same eager attention.

"Yes," she panted.

He released her peaked flesh with an audible pop.

"Be sure, Autumn. We have time."

Maybe, he did. She boiled out of control to have him inside of her. She nodded.

"I'm sure."

With her still in his arms, Rui stood.

"Hold on, sweet."

She wrapped her legs tight around his lean hips. Crossing her ankles, she locked her heels together atop of his toned backside. With her chin resting on his shoulder, she had a nice view of muscles.

Autumn balled her fingers into a fist and fought the urge to run her hands over every ounce of flesh she could reach.

Then, the ring of a cell phone cut through the air.

"Damn it," Rui muttered under his breath.

"Don't answer it," she said. She was so close to having him, she didn't want anything to come between what was about to happen.

"It might be Simone's school."

She lowered her head, embarrassed by her selfish behavior. Rui was a father, first. Of course, he should answer his phone. Wise up, Autumn, she thought. The man's a single father. He can't play hooky to get some nooky.

"Rui Conners," he spoke into the receiver.

Instantly, Autumn knew something was wrong. Rui radiated tension, the air seemed to crackle with it.

"Kirsten," he said, his tone soft, no longer with the huskiness he had with her. "What is it? What's wrong?"

The ex-wife. Rui's tone, one of concern and something more she couldn't quite identify, registered like a spill and tumble down a hill. She didn't like it.

From her position, Autumn couldn't see his face, but she heard the passion of the moment leave his voice. The burning desire surging through her body cooled, the sensual marathon over before it began.

Lifting her chin, she whispered, "Put me down."

His mind on the woman on the other end of the phone, Rui released Autumn. He didn't offer an apology or glance her way when she slipped from the room. She felt tears prick the back of her eyes.

For a moment, she'd really believed he wanted her.

CHAPTER SEVEN

O ver the course of the next two and a half weeks, Autumn took to visiting Simone's classroom every other day in preparation for the mother-daughter tea. Kelby welcomed the extra pair of hands, and Autumn enjoyed the connection. Some of the kids had began their own playlists. Eager to use the techniques she learned about in class, Autumn encouraged the students to customize their song selections for different moods, from concentration while studying, or to relax before bedtime, to challenge frustration in a constructive way. To her surprise, Simone had started a journal where she recorded song lyrics. Happy with inroads she'd made with Simone, Autumn tried not to think about her employer.

Since the night of Kirsten's phone call, Autumn noticed a quiet storm had infused Rui's normally clam demeanor. In typical Rui fashion, he hadn't disclosed any details about the conversation with his ex-wife, but Autumn sensed a volcano roiling beneath the surface.

She tried to ease the tension in the house. One night, Autumn baked two batches of chocolate chip cookies, after she discovered three bags of the Keebler creations added to the pantry. Simone had smiled the entire week, her packed lunches now the envy of her classmates. Simone had even made a few friends. Autumn took pride in the bridge she'd helped to established between Simone and her peers, as well as her father. She looked forward to the soft smile on Rui's face when he walked through the door after a long day. She got the sense he genuinely liked having her around. As hard as she tried to fight it, she had begun to feel at home.

Also, now that her runs started from home and through the residential neighborhood, she had acquired a few encouragers and a part-time running partner. Tommy, a new executive at the 1St Bank had taken to joining her on her runs at least three times a week. Autumn found she enjoyed the company, especially on the thirty-mile runs she reserved for the weekend. She'd gotten into a weekday routine of prepping a little breakfast for Simone, running, packing lunches for all, and getting Simone off to school.

Rui strode into the kitchen, his long legs encased in tight denim, a light blue polo untucked. "We have the Scrabble board set up. You coming?"

Autumn groaned. "Ugh. Sure your self-esteem can withstand another Friday night whipping?" Her second day on the job, Rui had invited her to join in on family game night. Rui loved board games: Yahtzee, Monopoly, Trivial Pursuit. Of course, he wiped the floor with her and Simone when it came to history. Simone wasn't half bad at pop culture. Autumn discovered she excelled at music, art, and politics. Who knew? But, Scrabble...she'd pretty much accepted that she dominated at the game. Guess all those years locked in a room with her eyes glued to a book boosted her vocabulary.

"Give me a minute. I need to send one email, and then I'll join you at the torture table," she giggled.

Rui nodded and turned to leave, but then he asked. "Who?"

She quirked a brow in surprise. The question was out of character for him. They hadn't progressed to the hot and heavy petting like they had the day that Kirsten The Orgasm Killer called. Rui never failed to kiss her cheek or slide a hand around her waist when he thought Simone wasn't in the room watching their every move. The youngest Conners was smart, and Autumn doubted the girl missed any of the shared glances between the two adults in the house.

"One of my running partners." Tommy, though not the only runner in the community, was the most reliable. Especially with the grueling run Autumn planned to start at first morning light.

Rui leaned over and kissed her forehead. "Don't be long. I'll miss you."

She softened just at the words. "I won't."

Without much ado, Autumn typed a message to Tommy. Tomorrow's run would consume five hours of her day. She planned to whip up a protein shake for them both, and then tear up the pavement. Saturdays were lazy days in the household, with Rui and Simone slow to leave their bedrooms. With two sleepy heads, Autumn put every hour to good use. Truth be told, it would be nice to figure out what to do about Rui. The hope that their relationship would progress beyond a few stolen kisses seemed more like wishful thinking at this point.

Entering the dining room, she said, "All done," taking her seat at the table.

Rui centered the Scrabble board in front of him at the head, while Simone loaded her wooden shelf with square lettered tiles.

Autumn reached into the box lid, extracting the score sheets.

She looked across the table to find a devilish smile on Simone's face. "I'm going to kick your butt."

Autumn went to raise her finger.

"Sorry," Simone said preemptively. "I meant I'm going to beat the pants off your butt."

Rui stared at his daughter. "That's not any better, young lady. How's your journal coming along?"

Simone shook her head. "Fine," she beamed. "I made up a new song."

"That's awesome, baby girl. I'm so proud of you."

Autumn's heart did a back flip. Watching the interaction between father and daughter imprinted on her brain. Like a video recording, tonight would always be a special memory for her. This felt like a safe place to share her heart. She wanted this life, here with Rui and Simone.

"Daddy, how do you say I'm going to win? If I beat you, can I have an allowance?"

Autumn smiled. "You just did." She and Simone had come a long way in their interactions, much to Rui's relief.

"I'll buy whatever you need. Since when do you want your own allowance?"

Simone's brow wrinkled. "Oh, you're right," she said in reply to Autumn.

"See how easy that was?" Autumn lifted both hands, "Look, Mom. I said something nice and it didn't hurt one bit."

Simone shrugged. "I get it." Simone shifted her tiles as she spoke. "I want to spend my own money. Like Autumn," she said, not making eye contact.

Under the table, Autumn felt Rui's big hand on her knee. "Oh yeah? What are you going to buy?"

She tried to hide her smile when he inched his fingers up her thigh and squeezed. She might just lose this round but win big later tonight.

Simone smiled big. "Something expensive."

The game progressed at a fast pace. Rui was a brilliant historian, but playing a word game with him was like pitting his adding machine vocabulary against a smartphone with an international dictionary app. Yep, he'd been working on his vocabulary, but she managed to outscore Mr. Webster's protégé again.

"Autumn, look," Simone said pointing at the board. "Daddy lets you win."

His mouth dropped open. Turning to Rui, Autumn watched as red slowly crept up his neck. So, the little one was right? Here Autumn thought for once she had him up against the wall.

In a fit of incredulity, Autumn flicked her index finger off her thumb, and toppled the shelf housing her tiles.

"You sneak," she charged, sliding her thigh out of her reach.

Rui jumped. "Hey," he protested. "She's eight. What does she know?"

"Daddy," Simone cried. Out of her seat, she launched herself at Rui, who easily caught her. With his daughter cradled in his arms, he began to tickle her belly. Simone dissolved into a fit of giggles.

Autumn looked on in happiness. This was family. She felt lucky just to witness the sight of a father enjoying time with his child. A part of her wondered what it would be like to have a child with Rui, their child.

"Autumn," he called, their eyes meeting. "Come here."

She frowned, at first, wondering what he wanted with her. "Why?"

"You're not getting out of your tickle punishment."

"What...what did I do?"

He grinned. "Don't play innocent. You and the little one ganged up on me."

Lifting his hand, he gestured her forward. "Come on and take your punishment like a big girl."

"Yeah, Autumn. And since daddy helped you, I win," she cheered.

Rui raised two fingers on his right hand. "I plead the fifth."

"I get my red bottom shoes," she sang. "They expensive, they expensive," she chanted. "My red bottom shoes," Simone giggled, dragging out each word.

Autumn froze. What in the sugar plum fairy? How had she? When had she?

Rui shot a look of horror in her direction. Oh no, how had Simone heard *that* song? Heat blossomed under her skin, and Autumn felt beads of perspiration erupt on her forehead. Oblivious to the change in the two adults in the room, Simone laughed, the tone that of childhood innocence.

A concerned father scooped up his little girl, his face grim. "Where did you hear about the red soled shoes song?"

How had Autumn allowed this to happen?

Simone frowned. "What song? Some of the big girls were talking about how cool the shoes are. I want a pair," she said, a little whiny.

Rui visibly relaxed, his shoulders dropping away from his ears. Autumn breathed a sigh of relief.

"The answer is no." Rui's tone brooked no argument. Simone seemed to register there was not room to finagle a different answer.

"Okay," she said, a little too slow. Autumn could tell there was more to come. "So, can I still have an allowance?"

"If you help Autumn around the house-"

Simone started pumping her fist before Rui could finish.

"And, you stay out of trouble at school."

The fist pump was a little lower on that one, but her smile remained bright and happy.

"Alright, but Autumn still gets her punishment."

"Hey," Autumn chimed in, "leave me out of it."

"No way, Jose. Daddy finds all your tickle spots."

Autumn looked at Rui. Heat flashed in his eyes. Instantly her body reacted. She just bet he did.

IT was after nine-thirty when Rui tucked an exhausted Simone into bed and spread a little pink blanket with blue butterflies over her. She was still babbling she wasn't sleepy when he flicked the gown-shaped nightlight on in her room and closed the door. Now, that he'd tucked one baby into bed, it was time to do the same with the other. Except he wanted Autumn in his bed tonight. Torture was the only way to describe his attempt to go slow with her.

Back in the dining room, Autumn was placing the last of the games pieces back in the box and closing the lid when he entered the room. He closed his arms and leaned his hip against the corner of the table.

Looking up she gave him a shy smile before telling him, "Good night."

Before she could move farther away, he reached for her. Encircling his arm around her arm. "Hold up, Autumn."

She glanced down at his paler hand on her golden skin, and then looked up at him. Desire swirled in bright circles in those dark eyes. The air between them heated. Even without moving he could see his hands caressing her bare flesh. "How much longer?"

For a brief second, her passion-filled eyes rounded in confusion.

"What are you asking, Rui?"

Unable to bare the separation between them, he pulled her in closer, encircling both her upper arms so she now faced him.

"I don't want to take advantage of you...you're just getting your life on track again, but, I'm crazy for you, Autumn. Can't wait much longer to take you to my bed."

She drew in a quick breath as if his admission shocked her. She had to know not touching her drove him to the brink. Rui's body was constantly running a stress test. His heart beat wildly one minute, and then slowed to a near stop until he saw her again.

Their gazes locked and held.

"Rui, you can't take what I freely give to you."

Wow. Now it was his turn to take a breath. Instead, he stepped closer, pressing so close to her, she had to feel his growing desire for her.

"I want to make love to you until neither one of us can stand."

"Really?"

"Sweetheart," he whispered, pressing his lips to the sensitive spot just beneath her ear. "I want to tempt you until you can't think, taste you until you scream, and take you until the only name you can utter with any understanding is mine."

Autumn licked her lips. And Rui, about to explode, unleashed all the passion and frustrated restraint of the past weeks.

"I'm going to kiss you real slow and deep all night long."

He chuckled when her breath hitched. Anticipation of driving her over the edge tightened all his muscles.

She nodded. "Yes," she moaned, "slow and deep are two of my favorite four letter words."

Raising his hands from her waist, he framed her face in his hands and angled her head so they'd fit perfectly.

"You're sure?"

She licked her lips. "Completely."

Without another word Rui scooped Autumn up and into his arms. He pulled her in close until he felt her warmth against his skin, the rounded contours of her delectable curves softening against his hardness.

Though he knew he should probably slow down, he covered the distance to his bedroom in what felt like seconds. With his hands filled with willing woman, he used his foot to kick the door closed. Rui was focused on making Autumn his. He'd just about settled into the fact that Kirsten wasn't coming back, and he and Simone would forever be alone when Autumn got sucked into his life. Tonight, he'd show her how grateful he was to have her affection. Despite his best efforts, his mind made the next logical conclusion...marriage, children, a forever family.

Gently he laid her on his bed. Hoping she hadn't changed her mind, he asked, "Comfortable?"

"Yes," Autumn replied, propping herself higher on the single pillow at her back.

They shared a heated glance. For Rui, it was truly a life-changing moment to see a woman, this woman in his bed after years of a cold space being his only companion. In the morning, he'd wake to Autumn with his scent on her skin.

Reaching for him, she whispered, "Touch me."

He cupped her cheek, studying the angles of her face. "You're beautiful," he whispered before pressing his mouth to hers. He noticed an increase in the rise and fall of her chest.

With sure fingers, Rui reached for her blouse. A moment later, the first few buttons were loose, freeing the swells of her twin mounds. Eager to please her, Rui inhaled through the rush of blood rumbling in his veins. Slowly, he removed her clothing, first the blouse and lacy chocolate bra, and then the jeans along with a thong that barely covered the triangle of hair between her shapely thighs. Glancing down, he let his eyes soak in every detail in the slender line of her shoulders, the full breasts, trim waist, and womanly hips.

"Perfect," he whispered.

She smiled. "What's that?"

Lifting a hand, he stroked her hair. "You're perfect, Autumn."

A slow rise of color infused her cheeks. When she tried to lower her head, he stopped her.

"Don't shy away from my compliments. You'll get tired of hearing them...but, I love everything about you."

Her breath hitched.

Had he said the "L" word aloud? Yes...he felt the truth of the words in his heart. Having Autumn in his life meant more than keeping his heart safe. Rui trusted her with his two most precious possessions, his child and the rapid-beating organ in his chest. Autumn would cherish his love with more than just her body. He felt it down to his bones. What he had with Autumn was the real deal.

"Rui," she whispered. "You shouldn't say..."

"It's the truth." Looking into her face, he saw the hope flare in her eyes. The hope that she tried to hide from him. "I love you, Autumn."

Tears collected in her eyes. "Really...you do?"

Rui's heart clenched. How could anyone have hurt this beautiful woman?

"How can I not." He smiled. "You're everything I want in a woman. Beauty, brains, compassion, generosity and devotion."

She reached for him. In anticipation of what was to come, Rui pressed the magnetic closure on the headboard drawer. Autumn glanced over her shoulder, eyes intent on the three-pack of condoms clutched in his hand.

She sat up and grabbed them from his fingers.

"Three?"

"I bought more," Rui said joining her in the bed. "We'll start with these."

A nervous laugh escaped her lips. "Ambitious?" she asked.

"More like honoring a long-awaited gift."

He grabbed her hip rolling until they faced one another.

"Wrap your arms around my neck." Without hesitation, Autumn did as he instructed. "Do whatever you want to me. Just...," He paused, not wanting to sound as desperate as he felt. "Keep your hands on me," Rui said. He wanted her to know there were no limits.

Slowly she lifted her head, a wicked grin on her face. "I feel the same way, Rui. Whatever you want."

He growled low in his throat. "Never, sweetheart, tell me I can do what I want with you. I might not let you out of my bed."

She laughed. "I'm alright with that."

Man, did that make him harder than stone.

Autumn leaned forward and covered his mouth with hers. Rui let her tease and lick before stroking into her mouth and taking the lead. At first, she held back. When he tightened his hold, reassuring her that she was safe to explore, she did just that. He felt the bond of trust as her lips relaxed, her curves softened, and she melted into his body.

"That's it, sweetheart," he said into her mouth. "Let go."

He pulled her atop of him, twisting his bare hips between her spread legs.

"Rui," she breathed. "More."

"Shhh, we have forever," he gasped. Probably shocked with his use of forever, but it's how he felt. With his mouth, he slowly caressed her body. From her lips, to the slender column of her neck, he trailed wet kisses down to her twin peaks. Once there, he drew a taunt bud into his mouth. When she groaned his name, Rui's pressure spiked knowing that his style of lovemaking pleased her. After Kirsten left him, he started to question if he knew what the hell he was doing in the bedroom. But, the sexy little sounds of delight spilling from Autumn's lips reassured him that he did something right.

Feeling confident, he slid lower, licking a heated path over her abdomen, past her navel down to her hip bone. Her skin, so smooth and soft, begged him to mark her. He wanted nothing less than to devour her. Gripping Autumn around the waist, Rui lifted.

He heard the catch in her breathing when he nipped directly over her mound.

"I want to taste you."

He thought he might have shocked her, but then hungry lit her eyes, and a slow smile spread across her full lips.

With a slight tilt, she held still at the perfect angle. With his hands circling her thighs, he used his mouth to explore her.

With the first flick of his tongue, she cried out and he was addicted. Rui could barely think straight. Her taste was sweet and wicked, sacred and cursed wine. He was lost in her.

"Take me."

He plunged forward until she exploded, and her honeyed taste fell upon his lips.

Autumn was breathtaking in her release. Every inch of her was exquisite in her surrender, warm, soft, caring, and real.

Before she could recover, Rui lifted, and lay her down beside him. Immediately he covered her body with his.

"Rui...what..."

He didn't speak. With deft hands, he applied the condom and pushed forward.

"Ahhh," she moaned.

"Move with me," he ordered, barely able to speak.

She gripped his shoulders, and he relished the bite of her nails digging into his skin. Being joined with her like this, he never wanted it to end. Like he promised, he kissed her, teased her, coaxed her, till he was almost out of his mind.

"Please, Rui. More."

His name tumbling from her lips stroked his male pride. He watched her. Auburn curls covered his pillow, and he could scent a hint of milk chocolate in the air. Tiny beads of sweat formed in the area above her lip like a garden of wild flowers just starting to bloom. Warm breath escaped her lips to dissipate in the valley of his chest with each movement. With her hands she stroked his arms, his chest, and lower, urging him on. Did she realize how generous she was with her lovemaking? Autumn wanted to be taken, claimed. She knew he loved her, reverenced her body. There would be a time for gentle later.

"Hold tight to me."

She did, and Rui gave them both the ride of their lives. Driving hard, he pushed until they both hung on the edge of complete ecstasy, and then they fell into the swirling eye together.

"Yes, Rui," she cried out.

Pressing himself deeper Rui felt the pull of her delicious pulsing waves and he let go in, giving himself over to the blinding pleasure. Any past, his or hers, was annihilated in their spent passion.

Autumn gripped his face. "I love you, too."

Panting for breath, he said, "I think I'm the happiest man alive." He lowered his lips to her and ravished her mouth. He was in love with her...and she loved him too.

Hours later he asked, "Did I make you feel good?"

Beside him, Autumn shifted her head until their eyes connected.

"Hmmm, yes. I don't ever want to leave your bed."

Rui sipped at her lips, savoring the taste of her mouth. "Good. Cause I want you to stay in my bed and in my life."

Propped on one elbow, Autumn regarded him. "Rui."

"Yes, sweetheart," he said collapsing beside her on the bed, and pulling her into his side.

"I want to taste you now." Whoa. She wanted him after they had—after he'd been inside- "Yes, Rui. I want you just as you are."

As Autumn worked her way down his body, tasting him with her lips and tongue, life as Rui knew it forever changed. He'd sacrificed for his daughter, and now he'd do the same for this woman. There's nothing he would deny Autumn or hold back from her.

CHAPTER EIGHT

Sometime after four o'clock, Autumn was having the best dream. Rui had her pinned against-

"What you doing in my daddy's bed?"

Autumn bolted upright, to see Simone, dressed in Wonder Woman pajamas glaring with eyes wide. Rui, seconds behind her, scrambled for the throw at the foot of the bed, tossing it over Autumn's bare shoulders like a granny wrap.

While Autumn struggled to find her voice, Rui spoke up.

"Simone, go back to bed."

"No. Where's Autumn's shirt?"

This was a poignant reminder that Autumn's relationship with Rui would definitely impact the open access Simone had to his bedroom.

Autumn stilled, curious to how Rui would handle their newfound status...in love...with his daughter. Unease skirted down Autumn's spine. What if Simone refused to accept their love? Would Rui toss her aside like so many before him? No, she told herself, even as doubt crept in and pulled out a yoga mat, settled in for a long na-ma-STAY.

"Simone," Rui snapped with more authority than Autumn had ever heard in his voice when dealing with one of Simone's demands.

Instead, of responding with a healthy dose of apprehension, Simone crossed her arms. "Is Autumn your girlfriend?"

Whoa. Autumn could use some pointers from this child on the direct approach.

Rui shook his head in frustration. Of course, both of them were nude beneath the sheets. It's not like either of them could escort her from the room.

He looked to Autumn, as if searching for an answer. Autumn could see the strain reflected in the tight folds formed around his eyes.

"No."

Wait. Had she heard him right? Was this the same man who had professed his love to her...but after the actual act, he couldn't claim her.

"So, you and Autumn are not boyfriend and girlfriend?"

"I answered your question," he said, adding a warning that neither one of them could miss. "Now, out you go, Simone."

There had to be more he had to say on the subject. What about "Simone, I'm in love with Autumn. We're going to be a family." Darn it, why was he so quiet? Autumn looked to Simone. Ask another question, she thought. This time, Autumn wished the child had pushed for more answers.

The click of the door closing when Simone departed had Autumn waiting for an explanation. She sat still beside Rui, in stunned silence. What was one to say when love dimmed in the harsh reality of the day after the night to end all nights? This should have been the happiest day of her life. The man she loved, loved her right back.

"Rui," she began, having to ask him why he hadn't told Simone the truth.

"Wow," he looked over at her with equally shocked eyes, "I'll never leave that door unlocked again." He laughed, and then leaned over and gave her a kiss, deep and wet.

Autumn relaxed, so maybe last night would hold up to the burn of reality?

"Let's get dressed before she comes back."

Grinning, Autumn hopped from the bed, yelping when Rui gave her bottom a squeeze.

"You want to make an office call later today?" he asked, waggling his eyebrows.

Placing a hand on each hip, she posed. Delighted when Rui drank in an eyeful of her generous curves.

"You're being bad, professor."

Throwing back the covers, he rounded the bed, totally unaffected by his nudity.

"But, I'll be so good to you."

He certainly had been last night. When he took her in his arms, Autumn sighed.

"Hmm, come on, sweetheart. I have a very inquisitive eight-year-old with a stopwatch waiting."

He placed a quick kiss to her lips. "So, we do."

They walked into the kitchen twenty minutes later, side by side. Autumn would have liked to have Rui large hand holding hers in a show of solidarity, but maybe she was being a little naive.

Simone seemed to have regrouped, by the calculated look in her eyes.

"So, Autumn."

Uh oh. This was never a good sign. "Did you go to sleep in my dad's room all night?"

Very little sleep happened in her daddy's room. And Autumn hoped it continued, she was all kinds of sore and loving every sensation her body made her aware of.

"Simone," Rui interrupted infusing his voice with a calm that he obviously didn't feel. He inhaled deep, and Autumn saw that he'd made a decision. "You know how Autumn likes to make us feel better... with special cookies and stuff."

Where the heck was he going with this? She'd given him all the cookies and the jar last night. Hell, she was thinking about how to gather up the crumbs and present those, too. Rui had given her hope when she had none. He'd saved her when she'd been on the brink of being lost.

"Yeah, I know."

"Well, Autumn gave me something nice...just for me."

Gave him something nice? She gave her freakin' heart to Rui Conners. How could he deny what they had? Something nice like a pair of her old sneakers? She'd given him the best of her. It may have been childish, considering she wanted him to profess his undying love for her to an eight-year-old with the same passion that she felt, but...hey it wasn't everyday a man claimed to love her. A man who had gone out of his way to concoct a cockamamie story about Autumn and her helping hand tendencies.

Simone wasn't a child to take anyone at face value.

She looked to Autumn, who had stood, and placed her plate in the sink.

"So, you were helping my daddy...in his room?"

Autumn's hand clenched into a fist. Did Rui realize how much he'd hurt her by denying everything they'd shared last night? Did he plan to keep their relationship a secret from Simone...from everyone?

"You heard your daddy," she said. Autumn tried to keep the hurt out of her voice, but the sharp turn of Rui's head in her direction must have given something away.

"Simone, go grab your helmet. I'll take you for a bike ride."

Not we'll take you. She felt the push of her nose against the glass. Even after their night together, Autumn felt the thunk of hitting her head against that invisible barrier that kept her on the outside of everyone's life.

"Yes," Simone fist-pumped her arm. Disappearing from sight, the little interrogator left with a smile on her face. Autumn's happiness vanished with each passing minute as Rui's explanation to his daughter acted like tiny landmines, each one blowing open a dark crater.

Keeping her eyes averted, she walked past him. Time to put some distance between herself and this man. Mind set on escape, she looked not left or right, but straight ahead.

She jerked when Rui grabbed her waist, stopping her. His hold as firm on her skin as it was around her heart. God this hurt. Autumn didn't struggle because it was useless to try to break his hold.

"You okay?"

At this point talking was off the agenda. Distance and time would help. So, she said the words that held the quickest route to her goals. Out.

"Of course."

He looked down at her, those onyx eyes seeing what she refused to say. Autumn met his stare with a boldness she didn't feel. No, she felt weak. Weak for a man who had loved her so completely, she couldn't see her body without seeing his.

"Now, why don't I believe you?"

Well, that made two of them. She wasn't sure she believed what he said last night.

"Let me go, Rui."

His grip on her hand tightened. That had to mean something, right? No, his caring for others would always be there, but caring didn't mean love.

"No, tell me what's going on?"

Lifting her chin, Autumn ignored his question. With her feelings raw and the wounds of his words fresh in her heart and mind, now wasn't the time to expose this new vulnerability. There had been enough of that in his arms well into the night.

"I told Ivy I'd stop by." It was the truth. She'd planned to visit No Limit tomorrow, but today was as good as any.

She twisted her wrist. "Let go."

Again, he didn't release her, but held on tighter.

"Hey," he growled. "I love you."

She noticed the slight catch in his breath like the words were foreign, too new to be comfortable rolling off his tongue. Well, she didn't suffer with the same ailment. She had no intention of returning the sentiment. Once would have to be enough.

"I remember," she clipped. She would never forget.

Rui's eyes flashed with concern, and then a fixedly determined spark. He grabbed her face, his familiar hands warm and comforting against her skin, and then he kissed her.

Initially, she resisted the invasion. As he parted her lips with gentle, yet demanding strokes, the passion born of the night, burst through its cage running into the light of today. Slowly, he coaxed her into compliance. Knees weak, Rui pulled her in close, keeping her upright when all she wanted was the weight of him atop of her, pressing, and then driving deeper.

"I do," he breathed into her hungry mouth, "love you. She's eight. Her mom is gone. Be patient with us."

Autumn felt her heart softening, but then she heard Rui's denial on repeat in her head. She broke free.

"Rui, I have to go."

"After I drop Simone at gymnastics, I'll head for the office. Stop by later."

How convenient she'd become for him. Rui had become accustom to her 'ready to serve' attitude. Not this time. Last night changed everything, at least for her. Moving out of his embrace, Autumn grabbed her purse and keys from the counter.

"Can't. I'm helping someone else feel better," because she couldn't feel any worse.

RUI felt unease the moment Autumn walked away from him. Leaving him not just physically alone, no, her withdrawal ached like a doctor had cut him open and removed a vital organ, his heart, maybe. He would fix this. And wasn't that the running shoe kick to the gonads, he was always having to fix something he'd messed up with her. How many chances would she allow him? In his head he prayed this wasn't the last song in their play list. Last night, as he made Autumn his, of course, his brain conjured up plans for a future, that included wedding vows, promises of forever, and babies. At the thought of Autumn round with his child, Rui adjusted himself. His woman, his baby, and a little brother or sister for Simone to love...yes, that was their destiny. A part of him wanted to follow Autumn to Owen and Ivy's place. Instead, he dropped Simone off, skipped the office, and drove toward the Abel Burney golf course. He had two hours to plan his apology.

Jose Primavera, the proprietor of the construction firm by the same name pulled up along side him.

Rui, pulling his clubs over his shoulder, closed the trunk, and rounded his vehicle. "You going out?"

He asked more out of politeness rather than wanting the company.

"Nope, just need to hit something, really hard."

Rui chuckled, thinking about his morning with Autumn, and the hurt he saw in her eyes. "I feel you."

He rethought his plan to be alone. Maybe, he could use some new perspective on his relationship with Autumn. Everyone in Endurance knew Jose had a thing for Amelie Bishop, the curator at the museum.

"You, Rui?" Jose questioned.

Rui bristled at the doubt in the other man's voice. It's not like his life was perfect. True he had freeze-dried his life waiting for his ex-wife to realize the terrible mistake she'd made in leaving him and her daughter behind. Here recently, Rui was beginning to believe he was the one who'd made a mistake...for waiting for a woman who'd walked out of his life and never looked back.

"Don't need your prejudice, Jose," he snapped.

Through the open window, Jose raised both hands in surrender.

"Whoa, gringo."

The comment had the desired effect. Both men chuckled. "You're an ass."

Jose stepped from the car. "You name calling have anything to do with your nanny? Owen mentioned you've been acting pretty assy lately."

Rui pulled up short. Assy. Men don't act assy. He'd be sure to tell Owen that the next time he visited No Limit.

"Autumn's not the nanny," he growled. She was the woman he loved. Yes, she may have entered his home under the guise of caring for Simone, but if he was honest with himself Rui had wanted her the moment he saw her in No Limit Bar & Grille.

Jose used his index fingers to make a cross. "Back," he scoffed, "the power of Christ compels you."

Rui spun on his heels. "You coming or not?"

The sound of aluminum clubs clanging together sounded behind him.

"Geesh, you're grumpy when you're having woman problems."

Up ending a club, Rui closed his hand around the grip, and swung. "Who said anything about a woman?"

Jose shook his head. "You got it bad," he said dropping a ball, and positioning himself behind his driver.

It was time to change the subject. He was just about to take another swing when Abel Burney joined them.

"Gentlemen," he said. Abel was the oldest of the three, somewhere north of forty. Abel's son, Jamal was over eighteen, out of the house, leaving the bachelor free to date the Sports Complicated journalist, Julie Kratzner.

Rui lifted his head, losing sight of the ball he drove harder than run over shoes.

"You playing this morning?" Not that Rui had time for a full round, but nine holes might do him some good. Golf allowed a man to think, separate the jumble of thoughts running roughshod over his common sense. Shoot, Autumn was making him crazy. From the moment he'd touched her, he'd been running, eyes closed into a cement wall.

"No, I'm not here to play, dumb genius."

The burst of laughter from Jose, drew a few disapproving looks for the surrounding golf enthusiasts.

Rui narrowed his eyes on the club owner, not in the mood for playing. "Care to explain?"

"Yeah, I would," Abel said getting in his face.

"I'm waiting."

Rui saw the strain around his friend's eyes. His spine went rigid. This couldn't be good.

"What is it?"

"Just left my woman over at No Limit."

Rui scoffed, pissed that he assumed Abel's issue involved him somehow.

"Since you looked pissed, you should've stayed and worked it out."

Abel leveled him with a pointed glare. "Sounds like a man who should take his own advice."

A pit opened in Rui's gut. Autumn. This was about Autumn. Dropping all pretense of interest in the range, he turned to face Abel, shoulders squared.

"What happened?" he asked.

"Autumn happened, that's what."

At the mention of her name, his suspicions confirmed, Rui had his bag in hand, ready to drive to her.

"Wait," Abel snapped.

"She's upset. All the women," he turned to face Jose, "yours, too, are with her."

Rui didn't care who was there. He needed to get to Autumn.

"Rui, I heard the words "leave him" and "get out of there" a few times."

What the hay? "So, you let them all poison her against me?" he roared.

Instead of responding, Abel just stared, pissing Rui off more.

"Seems to me, you set yourself up without any help from the women."

He stepped into Abel's space. "You think to tell me what to do with my woman."

When Abel narrowed the distance, Jose jumped between them.

"Hang on, gringos. No fighting allowed."

Rui didn't move, just kept his eyes on Abel. "There's no fight, Jose," Abel said meeting Rui's gaze. "I think it's clear to me and the women that Rui's laying claim before sealing the deal."

Oh, he'd sealed all right. Every inch of Autumn's body bore his mark. Ready to correct Abel's false assumption, he opened his mouth, but then his phone buzzed. In the serene quiet of the green rolling hills, the unwanted interruption seemed even more intrusive, but it cut through the tension. Jose looked relieved when Abel turned and disappeared into the clubhouse. Fumbling with the zippered pocket on his jacket, he fished out the thing, punching the control key by accident. Kirsten's lyrical voice, the husky lilt of seduction that used to set his blood to boil, caressed his eardrum.

"Rui," she laughed. He could hear the smile, picturing the subtle upturn of her painted lips. "It's me, silly. Say something."

A picture of Autumn, asleep in his arms flashed in his brain like a Las Vegas sign. Autumn who loved him. Autumn who cared for him and Simone. Rui's heart began to beat faster. For Autumn, he thought...for us. Without a hint of remorse, Rui pressed the control key again, disconnecting the call. For us.

AUTUMN could see concerned eyes studying her. Julie, Amelie, Cherron, and Ivy were gathered around the kitchen table in the private quarters attached to No Limit.

"You had better stop playing Netty Crocker for Professor Conners," Ivy steamed.

Everyone's mouth fell open and Autumn was silently thankful that Owen and his five-year-old had made themselves scare. Cai was a voice recorder when adults were nearby.

Autumn frowned at the woman of the roundtable. "It's my job."

Cherron, her voice light with the familiar stammer she kept quiet to hide. "Your, your...job is Simone. Not, not letting her father dip his spoon in the, the batter," she said, nodding her head.

As the other women nodded their head in agreement, Autumn felt a wave of sadness strike her body. Even though she was seated, she felt like she was swaying on her feet. They were right, of course. She'd done what she always did. Overstepped her scope of responsibility. Simone needed her, but somehow Autumn had incorporated Rui's needs into her job description.

"Autumn," Ivy touched her hand. When she looked up she saw more than outrage, and concern in her friend's face, she recognized a shared awareness. "I know how you feel."

How could she? Had Ivy and Owen's attraction started with a whirlwind kiss, and then culminated in a night of freaky, hot butt naked sex? Had their morning come with a nosey eight-year-old demanding to know why she was in daddy's bed? She gave a laugh, drawing the attention of her friends.

"I'll be fine," Autumn reassured them all.

Julie spoke up. "You know the little blue house on Dodger Lane is available for rent."

The journalist had come to town a year ago she'd heard. The house on Dodger Lane with its white picket fence, flower garden, and covered porch would be perfect...for someone else. Yes, she'd used the money Rui paid her to catch up her bills. Which left just enough for a pack of Now & Later and a can of potted meat.

"Thanks...but," she told these women, who'd become more than friends. They were her support system. One she thought to never have. "I can't afford to leave."

Amelia slapped the table. "That's crap. You can stay with us."

Had it really come to this? Maybe, she'd jumped the gun sharing that her lover had denied everything between them. Clearly, she and Rui needed to talk. It was only fair that she tell the man she'd shared her body with how she felt.

"Let's not be too hasty." Too late for that she thought as an image of her tangled in Rui's arms danced in her head.

"No such th-ing," Cherron said. "You have options."

She couldn't leave Rui. He said he loved her. She loved him, too.

"Cherron's right. Maybe you should come stay here," Ivy offered. "Just for a few days."

"It could clear your head," Amelie whispered, a warm smile on her face. "Or if you want to make him jealous. I could send Kenny by your place."

All the women groaned. Kenny's expertise lay with collectibles. For some reason he was a few tools short in the romance department.

"I love Rui. You don't leave people you love." A sensation she hadn't felt in a long time gripped her heart. Hadn't a man whispered those same words to her before? A man she'd given her virginity. Quickly, Autumn shut her eyes against the pain.

Walker had come into her life at the most vulnerable time. At eighteen, Autumn had been a short girl with too many curves, too little confidence, and no one to protect her. When one of the guys on campus had cornered her in an unpopulated stairwell, it was Walker who'd saved her from the creep's nefarious intentions.

From that day forward, she and Walker had been inseparable. She'd worshipped at his altar...with her mind, body and soul. Eighteen months later when she found him in bed with her aunt, that love had continued. She waited on him to come to his senses until the day the two had exchanged wedding vows and Walker moved in. Heartbroken, she withdrew from her classes and found a room-for-rent near the

USD campus. Running and music had saved her sanity. She'd sworn never to allow herself to be hurt that way again. Six years later, she enrolled in school, loaded up her ratty belongings and even rattier car and headed for Endurance.

"Thanks for listening, but I should head home."

Another round of offers flowed between them, but Autumn politely declined them all. Friends and family should not be yanked into private drama. She had given Rui her love, but this time she would be more careful with her heart.

CHAPTER NINE

Rui slammed the door as he strode into the kitchen.

"Autumn," he called. A water pipe ruptured on Bragg Avenue just outside of the course. Traffic had flown at a wheelchair-bound snail's pace. By then, he had to rush to pick up Simone from gymnastics. He arrived at No Limit to find Autumn gone and a steaming plate of stinky eye from Ivy. Whatever Autumn had said, he could feel the pressure building in his chest. Had she decided to leave him?

"Autumn," he called again. Checking the family room, he spied the formal areas of the house to find them empty. Rounding the hallway leading past his office to Autumn and Simone's part of the house, he paused outside of her door and then knocked.

"Sweetheart," he whispered, "open the door." Her car was in the drive, so she had to be in there. He tried the knob. It was locked. Prepared to go out and search for her if need be, Rui heard her voice and paused. She was talking. She must have been outside on the patio and hadn't heard him knocking.

Rui thought to give her some privacy. Turning, he heard her laughter and instantly his heart felt lighter. They would be fine, he would make it so as soon as she finished the call.

"So, when can I see you again?"

Rui froze. The siren blaring in his ear was nothing compared to the grinding of his teeth. A man was in his house...with Autumn, behind a locked door.

She laughed again, this time the tone was gentle, soft, flirty. Rui didn't stop to think. He acted. Spinning, he pushed all his strength into the kick and landed a shattering blow against the door lock. Wood creaked, and then splintered.

Autumn's scream ripped through the room. A man, shorter, but fit, moved to stand in front of her. Perfect. Rui could murder him without hurting Autumn.

"Get out," Rui barked, keeping his eyes on Autumn.

Autumn shook her head as if trying to regain her wits.

"Rui, what is going on?"

"A man in your bedroom is definitely not going on. Not now. Not ever."

The guy still hadn't moved away from Autumn. Obviously, not sensing the danger he was in. "Hi, I'm Thomas Roe. I work-"

"Get out, Thomas Roe."

To the man's credit he stayed put. If he wasn't keeping him from his woman, Rui might have bought him a drink.

"No can do, professor."

"Do I know you?"

"I oversee some of the larger accounts down at the bank, so I know you."

"Okay, Thomas who oversees. This is the last time I'm going to tell you to get the hell. Out. Of. My. House."

"Not until I know Autumn is safe."

Rui growled. "She's safe."

"Says the man who kicks in doors instead of knocking."

"My house. My woman," Rui gestured to Autumn, before looking Thomas in the eye. "Meet me outside."

"Why?"

"Because you need a lesson on what happens when you enter another man's home to sniff around his woman."

"Tommy," Autumn said, touching his arm.

"Don't touch him, sweetheart," Rui growled, ready to unleash his temper. "I'm barely holding it together over here, so seeing your hands on him is going to earn the banker a major withdrawal from his account."

That seemed to have the would-be hero rethinking his position.

"Look, Rui," Tommy began.

"So now we're on a first name basis?" Rui asked, taking another step closer.

"Okay," Tommy shrugged. "We are not on a first name basis. I don't want a fight with you."

"Fight. Thomas you misunderstand. Autumn is mine," he rasped. "I don't have to fight for what's mine, but in your case, I want to."

The man threw up his hands in defeat. Pivoting he looked at Autumn. Rui wanted to pound him into the carpet for the once over he gave her body. The appreciation reflected in his eyes could light a runway.

"Autumn, you know where I am if you need me."

The comment elicited a growl from Rui. Never had he acted so out of control over a woman. Yes, he was possessive of everything and everyone he thought to be his, but even with that as an excuse, he knew if Thomas made a move to touch her there would be the need for a paramedic and the sheriff.

Mentally, Rui was prepared to meet out whatever was required to ensure Autumn, and Thomas and the whole damn world knew she was his.

"She won't ever need you." No. Tonight he'd tell Simone about him and Autumn, and then he'd take his woman to bed and show her again who she belonged to.

AUTUMN stared at her bedroom door...what was left of it. When he'd forced his way into her room, his big body transforming the feminine boudoir into a gladiator's arena, her first thought had been to run to him. But, the murderous expression on his face had stopped her. She needed to protect Tommy from her deny-me-three times guess you-re-not-my-boyfriend. The banker was gone, before not he gave her one of those looks that said, you-need-to-call that one eight hundred hotline number they post in women's bathroom.

Autumn knew Rui would never physically harm her, but her heart may very well take a beating if things between them remained the same. Now, Rui stood in front of the shattered mess like a caveman ready to take down a mammoth. This was no refined college professor glaring down at her with onyx eyes so bright, they burned with the amber glow of hot coals. He had acted worse than a Neanderthal with Tommy, yet she couldn't deny the heat sparking in her veins as he claimed her as his own. Pushing that aside, but maintaining her distance, Autumn stayed near the foot of the bed.

She fixed Rui in a hard glare. "I can't believe you did that to Tommy. I had no idea you were capable of being such a jerk."

Autumn couldn't believe what she'd just witnessed.

"Believe it," he stated, matter-of-factly. "Don't defend another man to me," he railed at her. "I'm patient, not a pushover.

It was then that Autumn realized he wasn't the least bit remorseful for having treated Tommy poorly. Okay, sleeping with Rui definitely changed the dynamic between them. If he couldn't explain her in his bed, how the hell was he to talk himself out of an inquiry about kicking in her door?

"Tommy is my friend. I'm not trying to manipulate you."

Rui gripped her waist and hauled her up against his solid wall of a body. Why, even while arguing, did his scent drive her wild?

"If your friends have balls, they had damn well stay away from your bedroom if they don't want them smashed under my boot heel."

Autumn pushed against his chest, knowing the contact would only mute her brain and they needed to have this conversation.

"Rui, that's not fair."

He threaded his fingers through her hair.

"I love you. Fighting dirty is just the beginning of what I will do to keep you."

Autumn couldn't hear this right now, not after his repeated denial. Jesus could do it with Peter, but Autumn was far from being a disciple. When she tried to look away, he captured her chin.

"Don't make promises, Rui-"

"I love you, damn it."

She began to struggle in earnest. No way would she allow him to pull her in again.

"Stop telling me things you think I want to hear, Rui."

This time he released her.

"I'm a man, not a boy trying to get into your pants."

She smirked. "Too late for that."

He gripped her wrist. "I'm not playing you. Dang it, woman. I said I love you last night. I was inside your body."

She shivered at the reminder.

"So, forgive me if I'm a little pissed off to one, learn your friends are telling you to leave me, and two, I come home to find the woman I love with another man in her bedroom?"

"What does it matter, Rui?" She shook her head, so over the fighting. Walker had done the same the first time she confronted him about how chummy he seemed with her aunt. "We slept together. It doesn't have to be more."

"It is," he roared. Grabbing her up he kissed her. And because she knew if she placed what they had in a box it was the only way she would survive when this thing between them ended she kissed him back.

"I'm so sorry, Autumn," he stroked into her mouth. "Swear, I'll tell the whole damn world you're mine before I lose you."

Refusing to acknowledge his declaration, Autumn kept kissing him.

That is until she heard the distinct sound of someone clearing their throat. Had Tommy come back? Or worse, had Simone been dropped off, and now stood with her inquiring minds spy glass pointed at Autumn's eyeball. Talk about the ant under a sun heated magnifying glass, ouch.

She jumped but didn't make it very far because Rui kept an arm around her waist. They both swiveled to face the door.

"Who are you?" Surprise heightened Autumn's voice.

A woman with pin-straight ebony tresses floating above her shoulders watched them. Tall and willowy, the ebony beauty looked straight off Rodeo Drive or a fashion runway. She wore a scoop neck buttery cream-colored dress that barely reached mid-thigh, yet somehow managed to look tasteful as she balanced on pointy-toed candy apple red bottom heels that Autumn was sure belonged in a big-tent stilts routine. Her features had to be the envy of gods. Exotic smoke gray eyes, high cheekbones, and full lips accentuated her perfect size four figure. She looked like...money, Autumn thought. Lots and lots of hundred-dollar bills. Feeling inadequate in her running tights and sweat-wicking tee, Autumn resisted the urge to fidget.

"Kirsten?" Rui said, eyes fixed on the cover model for Cosmo magazine.

His voice was equal parts awe and anger. Autumn studied the woman. She looked composed, in control, like she was used to commanding minions and having her wishes fulfilled. Odd, Autumn had the strangest feeling that she'd seen this woman, not a likeness before.

"I waited until the arguing stopped."

Her voice was like a siren's song. Even now, Autumn's thoughts were crashing into each other, clamoring about Rui's possible connection to this regal specimen of womanhood.

"How did you get in here?"

Autumn noticed the tension in Rui's arm. Gone was the lover, the professor, this was definitely the fighter, but which side was he on.

"Wait...who are you?"

"Oh, I'm being rude." The woman extended a hand to Autumn. "I'm Kirsten Connors." Drums started to beat a constant Jumanji, you're about to be attacked by flying monkeys, kind of rhythm. And then the gray mist-eyed diva confirmed Autumn's worst nightmare. "Rui's wife."

The woman had the audacity to bat her lashes before giving Autumn a playful wink. What was this...taunt your husband's mistress move? "And you must be the woman Simone got arrested."

At that, both she and Rui frowned.

"She was never arrested. And, how could you know that?" Rui demanded.

Kirsten stepped across the threshold, like she owned the place. Did she? Autumn had never thought to ask her boyfriend any questions about his arrangement with the ex. When the woman, circled Rui's bicep in one well-manicured hand, Autumn had to fight the urge to snatch him away. Rui sensing her burning stare, moved beyond her grasp, yet he was no closer to Autumn's side.

"Simone wrote it in the letter asking me to come for her little tea ceremony," the woman sang, and Autumn swore she'd heard the voice before, though this was her first acquaintance with the competition. Then Autumn took a closer look, she knew this woman. Heck, the whole world knew her voice. Autumn's throat all of a sudden felt dry, while her palms began to sweat. Aria Arie the famous jazz and neo-soul songstress stood in front her.

"You're Aria," Autumn stammered. "The sin—singer," she managed to get out.

Neither Rui nor Kirsten responded. He was too busy scowling at the other woman's sultry smirk. How did she do it, look cunning and keel over gorgeous at the same time?

Kirsten gave Rui a wink. "Now husband, when you get through tickling the help, we need to talk."

Then Kirsten Conners exited the room leaving both Autumn and Rui in a tailspin. His wife, an internationally-known recording artist, was back. And yes, this was one more thing they needed to clarify, but Autumn couldn't help thinking how long it would be before she had to pack her bags...again.

CHAPTER TEN

Rui stood facing Autumn. She wouldn't meet his eyes. What was Kirsten doing back in Endurance? Simone had written his ex-wife dozens of letters in the year, none of them had prompted her to come home in the past. No, Rui knew the woman who'd owned his heart all those years ago. Kirsten's return had everything to do with Autumn being here. Now if he could get Autumn to look at him, maybe he could explain a few things about his former wife. Kirsten being in Endurance spelled troubled for Rui and Autumn. Rui's protective instincts kicked into high gear. He would keep Autumn and Kirsten apart. Knowing Kirsten, she'd be bored by the end of the week. When had his hopes for him and Kirsten's reconciliation been replaced by a future with Autumn? Rui shook his head. The moment Autumn came to Simone's aid with Mrs. Glatt she captured a piece of his heart.

He watched as Autumn pulled a clean shirt and leggings from a dresser drawer. She remained silent. He wasn't sure if she was gathering her thoughts or keeping him from knowing hers at the twisted turn of events.

"Autumn, sit down, we need to talk," he said pushing away from the door.

She glanced up at him. " I don't have time to talk. Simone will be home soon. I need to get dinner on the table."

When she turned toward the ensuite bathroom, he crossed the room in three quick strides, blocking her exit.

"I'll take us out to dinner."

Rolling her eyes, she gave an incredulous laugh, the sound harsh and strained.

"No thanks," she snapped. "I'd rather lick a pig's foot than join you and your ex for dinner."

He grabbed her around the waist. "Hey," he rasped. "Kirsten being here doesn't change anything with us."

She shoved at his chest. Rui didn't budge. Instead he pulled her closer, not surprised when she used the ball of clothes in her hand to keep from touching him. He got it. Kirsten's arrival unsettled him, too. Heck, finding Autumn with Tommy had him ready to spit venom.

"Rui." She breathed his name as if he was the most naive man on the planet. "So, you want me to join you and your family at your first dinner together in more than a year? Seriously, professor?" she asked, a hint of sarcasm in her voice.

He lowered his head till their mouths were almost touching. "What I want is for you to be patient while I get to the real reason for Kirsten's visit."

Autumn dropped her head onto his chest. The sensation of her resting against him was heady, and Rui said a prayer of thanksgiving for this small gesture of trust.

"She told us already," Autumn whispered. "She's here because Simone wants her mother to attend the mother-daughter tea, not me."

The hurt lacing her words threatened to bring Rui to his knees. Without thinking about the possible rejection, he pressed his lips to hers. Using his tongue, he swept across her lips before pushing deep inside. Her mouth softened beneath his. She eagerly drank from him, and Rui let himself drown in her flavor. Autumn tasted even sweeter. She nipped at his lip and the sting shot straight below his belt.

"Nothing," he growled, "will change between us."

For a brief second, Autumn's body stiffened, her kiss less intense. Rui appreciated that his woman needed to be convinced that he spoke the truth. Lowering his head, he stopped at her chest. Her breathing was labored, and he recognized he was in similar shape. Without looking up he captured one taut peak between his teeth and sucked. Ripples of equals parts need and want vibrated through Rui. He lifted Autumn into his arms and walked them back to the bed.

"I love you, Rui."

Things happened quick after that. Shoes kicked off, belts loosened, clothes dropped, and then he entered her. Perfect. He could stay inside this woman forever.

The last coherent word he remembered before a pleasure so intense ripped through his body was, "Love you too," he grunted out. "Nothing changes. I promise," he whispered.

He loved Autumn. Kirsten being in Endurance would not tear them apart. Rui would prove his words true if it took all night.

THE next morning Autumn awoke to find herself alone in bed. Rui hadn't spent the night with her, nor had he invited her to his bed. After their make-up session, he'd left to pick up Simone from school. Kirsten had joined him. Autumn had tried not to feel abandoned. Alone, she'd taken a quick shower, washed a load of laundry, and prepared dinner, a light fare of blackened salmon steaks, sautéed zucchini, and smashed carrots. Two and a half hours later the happy family, Rui, Kirsten, and Simone walked through the door, all smiles with No Limit take-out containers in their hands.

"Autumn, look," Simone said, running up to her. Autumn could practically reach out and touch the excitement sparking around Simone. She could only imagine what it felt like to have her mother back after years of absence. While she lived with her aunt, her mother's visits had been few. Thinking back, Autumn now believed the rare occasions when she did see her mother were well-orchestrated. The visits, though spotty, never happened around significant events like holidays, birthdays, or graduations. Her mother made sure Autumn never got her hopes up about a reunion. "My mom brought me a real diamond necklace."

Simone fished around the collar of her shirt and then held up a thin yellow gold chain. Autumn placed her now cleaned plate in the sink. Wiping her hands on a dish towel, she bent at the waist. A diamond solitaire, maybe a quarter of a carat dangled between the eight-year old's fingers. Wow. The stone sparkled brighter than a celestial being. Clarity be damned. There were so many colorless facets to the stone Autumn could see her reflection.

"It's beautiful, Simone. Just like you," Autumn heard herself say. In an odd twist, Autumn found that she was happy for Simone. Little girls needed their mommies. There was a time when she would have prayed for a second chance with her mother. Looking at Rui, she acknowledged if Kirsten stayed, she would have to go. She'd stood then, speechless, but watching Rui. Their eyes met, and she noticed his smile had slipped away. So, this was his real life with his real family.

"Thank you. My mom said I could wear it to the mommy-daughter tea on Friday."

She flinched. Rui noticed and took a step towards her. She held up a hand to stay him.

"Autumn, let me help you," Rui said.

"Are you okay?" Kirsten asked. Oddly enough, her concern sounded genuine.

"I'm fine," Autumn breathed, shoring up her spine. "That's great news, Simone." So, this was how it was going to be. She'd been uninvited to Simone's tea. Autumn sighed. What had Kirsten called her? The help. Yep, for the first time since moving in with Rui, Autumn felt like he'd paid her for a service he no longer needed.

She went to her *quarters*. A part of her wanted Rui to come to her bedroom, even though she'd locked the door. Sleep claimed her some five hours later, well past midnight. Autumn lied to herself. She hadn't lain awake for Rui, nope. Sleep merely alluded her until reality took over. He wasn't coming for her.

The morning was unusually cool. Or, maybe it was Autumn running hot. This morning's run had been painful. Tommy hadn't joined her, and the kitchen had been a mess when she returned home. Was this still her home? Her heart sank at the possibility of having to leave?

"Good Morning," Rui said when she entered the kitchen. He handed her a cup of coffee. She accepted his peace offering and went to sit at the long couch they used instead of chairs on the end of the breakfast nook. Even the warm brew did little to thaw the cold clinging to her bones. Today fell real short in the good department. His eyes danced around like he was unsure where to start. "About last night."

"Don't worry about it. Salmon is great as a leftover."

"Kirsten said she wanted to talk about Simone. We ended up at No Limit for dinner."

Autumn pasted on a smile. "You don't have to explain." Actually, she didn't want to hear it. Old memories started to surface. She remembered the morning her boyfriend walked in the kitchen holding her aunt's hand. She hadn't wanted an explanation then either.

"It just happened to that some of the locals recognized her," he trailed off. "Time slipped away."

"I understand," she said, taking a sip of her coffee. She choked, sputtered, and then swallowed. The aroma was pleasing, but the liquid tasted worse than the bottom of a burnt rice bowl.

Rui closed the distance between them, snagging the cup from her hand. "That's Kirsten's special blend. I should've warned you."

And so, it begins. Could Rui be right? Was Kirsten's return an indication that she wanted back in Rui's life? Had they talked last night? Had they kissed or worse, consummated their reunion? She searched his face, looking for a sign of betrayal. Not that she'd recognize the bullet before it shot her between the eyes. She hadn't back at home.

"Stop fawning over me, Rui," she hissed.

He dropped to his knees at her feet. Tracking longs fingers through his dark mane, she stared at him.

"You're different, Autumn." Yeah, well, that applied to both of them. "You look at me like I'm going to hurt you. Like I already have. Nothing has changed for me."

"Rui, wake up. Your ex-wife is living in the house with us. She's rich, yet she's here."

"There are no hotels in Endurance. What was I supposed to do? Kick her out of her own house?"

How could she respond to that? It was Autumn who was the intruder.

"Daddy," Simone said, entering the room.

When she saw her father on his knees she stopped. Looking between the two of them she frowned.

"Autumn, are you still going to help my daddy in the bedroom now that my mommy is back?"

It probably would have hurt less if it had been a bullet. Of course, she couldn't continue to share Rui's bed.

"Yes."

"No."

She and Rui spoke at the same time. Simone confused by the opposing answers, looked to her father for clarification.

"Autumn and I need to talk about our arrangement."

Ugh, it sounded so illicit. An arrangement. Yep, the money exchange popped back into her head. Autumn just wanted the house empty, so she could think.

"Simone, grab your backpack. It's time for school." She looked at Rui. "Don't be late for your first class."

He stood to his feet. "I'll drop Simone off, and then come back here. You and I have to talk, Autumn. I don't want us to change."

"You already have, Rui."

Ten minutes later she was alone with her first cup of coffee, one that didn't taste like the bottom of her old running shoes.

"You like sleeping with my husband?"

Her head shot up from the cup she'd been putting to her lips. Kirsten wore a smoky blue silk robe, that gaped open at the neckline revealing too much of everything. What if Simone had seen her on display like this? Her feet were in yet another pair of red bottom high-heels with what looked to be real-fur across the toes. What that heck? Who could compete with gray eyes, flawless skin, and uninhibited sensuality?

From her position on the buffet couch, Autumn faced off with Kirsten.

Kirsten shrugged. "Rui's a great lover," she laughed. "I thought since we've both had him, you just last night," she said with the raise of a brow, "it was a safe topic."

Where was Kirsten trying to take this conversation?

"It's not. What happens between me and Rui is not up for public discussion."

Kirsten stood, crossed the floor, her impossibly high heels clicking like rain on a tin roof.

"We could make beautiful music together," she brushed one finger over the cap of Autumn's shoulder. "You, me, and Rui."

Whoa. Autumn recoiled. She hadn't seen that coming.

"You touch me again," she growled, the sound feral. "Your head is going to make contact with some hard rock. You feel me?"

Kirsten just smiled. "No need to get physical," she said licking her lips. "Not yet, any way. Rui and I have an understanding when I'm in town. I don't mind sharing him. Aren't you the least bit intrigued?"

Autumn didn't know what to make of Rui's ex-wife, but she knew it was time to go. In reality, the ball of anxiety that formed in her stomach last night grew into a full-blown atomic nucleus, unstable and ready to explode. Her dream of belonging to a family of her own, building a life with Rui and Simone had been a fantasy.

"No." When Autumn stood to leave, Kirsten called out.

"Just think about it. He wants you and I-well, I want you both."

Autumn looked Kirsten square in the eyes. "I don't have to. Tell Rui..."

"Tell him what, feisty little Autumn?"

Patronizing witch. Autumn was of the mind set to snatch one of Kirsten's mile-high stilettos off her foot and clobber her with it. Bloody shoes, indeed.

"He can take this job and shove it," she paused, "well, you know the rest."

Kirsten stood, her mouth slack with shock. It was petty, Autumn knew, but a sudden surge of relief flooded her at not being the only one caught off guard. She never would've guessed a song title could be so therapeutic.

RUI walked into his house with one goal, to talk with Autumn. When he entered the kitchen, Kirsten sprang to her feet.

"Hello, darling," she said.

Rui took in the outfit she wore, what little there was to the night robe.

"Put on some clothes on, Kirsten. I don't want Simone to ever see you dressed that way."

God, there was a time when he would have been chomping at the bit to get her out of those clothes. Now, he was a father with a little girl to protect.

"Simone is a beautiful girl. Men will eventually notice her," Kirsten reasoned.

Her lack of motherly protectiveness stung him. Rui remembered that Kirsten could be self-centered, but she had to understand young girls should not be made to dress like grown women, right? He wanted to shield his daughter for as long as possible.

"Not any time soon, so cover up while you're here," he said.

Kirsten came to stand in front of him. The scent of her expensive perfume wafted up to his nose, a mix of flowers, jasmine he thought. He didn't like it.

She smoothed a hand over his shirt. "There was a time when you loved seeing me in even less," she whispered.

Rui stepped back, but Kirsten followed. This time she locked her arms around his neck.

"That was before you left me for a life in the spotlight," he hissed.

Why was he even talking about this? Kirsten wasn't going to change, but he had. Autumn and Simone were his priority now.

"That's the past, Rui. I'm back and I want you in my life."

The hairs on the back of Rui's neck stood at attention. Where was Autumn? The last thing he needed was for her to overhear or walk-in on this scene.

"We have a child together. That's the only connection we'll have from here going forward." Rui reached up, gripping both of Kirsten's hands. The feel of her against his body felt wrong. He wanted Autumn.

"Don't be silly."

Rui smirked. "I'm not anymore. What we had doesn't work for me. Truthfully, it never did."

Her playful rouse slipped. "Trust me, Rui. We can make it work this time. Simone is older. You've had a successful career like you wanted. Now, we can enter the next phase of my career together, like a family."

Kirsten had gotten even better with her word games, but Rui had learned a thing or two from his ex-wife.

"Like a family?" he questioned. Kirsten would never settle for being a wife and mother. Rui saw that now that she was back in Endurance. "What is it that you really want from me, Kirsten?"

Instead of answering, Kirsten released him, stepped back and opened her robe. Rui was temporarily transfixed. Her body had changed. She was leaner, more defined, yet not as real. She seemed almost mannequin like.

His Autumn was a fluid poetry of smooth valleys and compact curves. Her body was a soft cushion to his hardness. Autumn was right; co-existence for the three of them under this one roof ended today. Kirsten needed to pack.

An audible gasp sounded in the room. Rui pushed Kirsten away, and spun on his heel. Autumn stood in the entryway, a suitcase in hand, and a duffel over one shoulder. Rui frowned. What was she doing? Why would she be carrying luggage?

"What are you doing with suitcases?" he demanded. Autumn glanced at Kirsten standing there with her robe open, her trim body on display. "Kirsten," he growled, "cover yourself."

Rui watched Autumn's face harden before going blank. What in the green hell was going on?

"I'm leaving," Autumn said meeting his eyes. "Looks like I picked the perfect time to put some distance between me and you two."

"No, no, Autumn. You can't leave, sweetheart."

"No, you can't," Kirsten interrupted. "Rui just asked me what I wanted. I was about to tell him, you."

Rui's brain short-circuited. What in the hell had Kirsten just said?

SO, Rui and Kirsten had an open-door marriage? Or was it ex-marriage? Whatever. Autumn left Rui and his freaky wife in the kitchen and walked out of the house.

Rui came after her. Autumn kept loading her car, shuffling bags to ensure her meager possessions fit. "Wait a minute. Damn it, Autumn. Don't put another thing in that car."

"No can do," she said closing her trunk.

A moment later, she found herself spun around. She looked up to see Rui's onyx eyes filled with worry, anger, and maybe fear.

"Kirsten is leaving, Autumn. Don't do this, please. You know I want only you."

Autumn wanted to believe him, but it was too little, too late. She'd traveled too far down this road before...recently. When her aunt and her ex- tied the knot, Autumn wanted to appear the bigger person. She'd thought love and family were more important than her feelings. How wrong had she been? Eventually, they all grew to resent each other. No way would she put herself in that situation again. A clean break from Rui and his baby mama drama was best.

"Your life is more complicated than mine. Three weeks ago, I would've handled this differently, Rui. But, I trusted you with my heart and my body."

"And you still can," he plead. "I love you, Autumn."

She shook her head, convinced that Rui believed every word he'd spoken. But, he also wanted the life he and Kirsten could have had.

"Rui," she sighed, "I was a trial run until your Hollywood special came home." She grappled to find the right words. "I can't be a substitute wife. Not even for you."

"No, Autumn," his tone one of rising panic. "I'm not asking you to be a stand-in for Kirsten. You walking away, this isn't you."

Autumn recoiled at his assumption. What did he know about her. She knew his life, what did he know about what she wanted out of life. After all, she got paid to make his life easier, not the other way around.

"Rui, you don't get to say that to me," she grabbed her suitcase. "I was happy," she screamed. "You did this," she charged. "You broke us," a sob escaped, "for her."

Surrendering to another man was a path she could not afford to tread again.

"I want to be the man you need." She could hear the pleading in his voice, that little nudge for her to conform to his will. "I'm teachable. I promise," he paused, "I'll make this better, but–,"

And there it was, the part where she was supposed to cave in.

"I want, no-," she said, feeling the ball of anger swelling inside her, "I deserve a man that will go the distance for me, who'll make me his priority."

"I am," he started to say more, but Autumn turned accusing eyes on him. How could he think keeping Kirsten in this house, with her, was putting her first?

"You are a handsome liar, Rui Conners."

"You have to give me more time to fix this. You know I love you, but Kirsten just got back. Simone needs to-,"

"No," she hissed. "The man who will love me forever, would never ask me to wait. This situation with Kirsten hurts me, Rui."

When he just stood there, a mask of defeat on his face, she knew. It was time to go.

"I want you here."

She nodded. "I know. And the fact that you refuse to acknowledge why I can't stay, tells me you're the wrong man for me."

Her fantasy of a sweeping love affair that crossed the finish line with a marriage proposal ended with her car packed and pulling out of Rui's driveway. With one last glance over her shoulder, Autumn punched the gas pedal and drove away from the man she'd fallen in love with.

CHAPTER ELEVEN

Rui opened the door to his bedroom needing an acetaminophen tablet, a bath, and a drink. Had he really done what Autumn accused him of? Wooed her, seduced her, and then discarded her when Kirsten arrived. Either way, he'd made a big mess where his woman was concerned. First, he needed to get rid of Kirsten, and then figure out a way to bring Autumn home.

He flipped on the light to find his ex-wife in her birthday suit.

"I thought you'd never come to bed," Kirsten crooned.

Black stilettos covered her feet and her hair flowed over on his pillow. The pillow he'd used to cradle Autumn's head.

"Kirsten," he let the exhaustion seep into his voice. "I told you to stay away from me."

"And," she leaned forward, pushing her cleavage higher, "I heard you, but, I decided against it."

"I don't want this," he said pointing to her nude body. "Not now. Not ever."

"Since when, Rui?" She began to crawl towards him, a sly smile on her painted lips. "We both know you've been waiting on me to come home."

The fact that she knew he'd waited for her to realize he and Simone needed her grated. Well, they had moved on-he had moved on. He loved Autumn.

"Your being here is confusing everything."

"No one is confused, Rui. You wanted to play with the nanny. I don't have a problem with you scratching an itch. I wouldn't mind a taste of her too."

He backed away, disgusted he'd ever been attracted to this woman. "She's not the babysitter. I'm in love with her."

Kirsten scoffed, giving up all pretense of seduction. Back propped against the headboard, she covered her ample chest with both arms.

She met his glare. "Yes, I can imagine," she smirked. "You and Tommy so eager to run to her defense, apparently."

Rui balked at the insinuation that Autumn was playing both men.

He laughed. "Every woman doesn't manipulate her man, Kirsten." Turning he walked to the door. "Pack your stuff. I want you gone within the hour."

He heard her move, but he kept moving toward the exit. "What about Simone?"

"I'll tell our daughter that you left."

The sound of the front door opening and closing snapped him out of his newfound hell. How could he have driven Autumn away?

"Daddy. Autumn," Simone yelled through the house.

His daughter had transformed from a petulant kid to a well-mannered little girl who, on occasion, still shouted at the top of her lungs.

Not turning around, he called out. "I'm here."

To Kirsten he said. "I'll handle this. Get dressed and packed," he paused a bit. "In that order."

"Mr. Jose said I can ride home from school with Lupita anytime."

His daughter had actually made a friend. Realization of Autumn's impact in their lives drove home the fact that he was a fool. He should have begged her to stay. Instead he made excuses for why she should wait on him.

"We'll see," he called. "I'll meet you in the kitchen." Seconds later he was seated at the table when Simone entered the room. With her over-shirt tied around her waist, she went to remove her backpack, then thought better of it. God, Autumn had changed them both.

"Where's Autumn?"

He had no idea how Simone would respond to Autumn's absence. If the sick feeling in his gut was any indication, he was in for a long night of restlessness. He'd drive over to No Limit and talk her into coming back home.

"Come here," he said pulling out the chair next to him. "Sit."

Looking around the kitchen, she sniffed the air. "What's for dinner? I hope Mom isn't going to try to make us drink that dirt, grass, and berry stuff again."

Rui mirrored his daughter's frown. "No honey. No flaxseed spinach smoothies tonight."

"Then, why isn't Autumn cooking? We going out?" Simone took a hesitant step toward the chair he offered.

"I need to talk with you about something that happened while you were in school."

"Okay, but I have to practice. Tonight is the last night for me to get all my dance steps right."

"I know. That's what I want to talk with you about."

"Wait," Simone said, her small hand still on the chair back. "Did Mom leave?"

Simone's eyes reddened.

He crossed the room and pulled his little girl into his arms. He thought she would protest, instead she hugged his waist tight.

"I knew she would leave us. She does not love us daddy, not like Autumn."

He scooped her up in his arms, holding her tight until he felt her head settle on his shoulder.

"Shh, honey," he soothed. "Your mom loves you and, she didn't leave us."

"Then what's wrong, Daddy?"

"Your mother is moving out."

When Simone didn't respond, Rui turned his head to get a better look at her face. "Did you hear what I said?"

"Yeah," she sniffled. "That's okay. This way Autumn can be happy again."

At the mention of Autumn's name, the bottom fell out of Rui's stomach. Even his eight-year-old realized he'd hurt Autumn with his stupidity.

"There's more?"

Simone lifted her head, using the hand stamped with a smiley face to wipe her tears away.

"Daddy," she protested. "Autumn's going to make me do the waltz first if I'm late."

"She won't," he whispered.

Simone smiled, "Yeah, you're right. When she sees I earned my third Good Apple Award two weeks in a row, she'll forgive me. I would've had three if-"

"I know, that boy was asking for it?" he repeated the argument he and Autumn sat through when the incident first happened.

She got animated, arms opening wide. "Told him to leave me alone. I tried to turn the other cheek like Autumn said, but he'd pushed me too far."

Rui could see his error clearly. Like that bully with Simone, Autumn had endured enough of Rui taking her love for granted.

"Simone," he cut in, "Autumn is not here."

"When is she coming back?" she said, cheer in her voice.

"She's not?" Not on her own accord, Rui thought.

"What...why, Daddy?" Simone's eyes started to tear up.

"Autumn's going back to her old job," he offered, trying to show a brave face.

"She can't. She liked it here before Kirsten came. She wanted us."

Simone studied his face for an instant, seeing the pain he'd caused etched on his face. Her arms dropped, and the smile fell away.

The tears he thought were done flowed freely over his daughter's cheeks. "Why," she sobbed. "What did we do, Daddy?"

Dear God, his child didn't deserve any of the blame. The fault lay with him. He'd betrayed Autumn's trust. He'd selfishly tried to hold onto his past, while telling Autumn she was his future.

"Shh, baby," he said, his voice cracking. "You didn't do anything wrong."

"I did cause Autumn said when you love somebody you stay with them, you fight for them."

And that's exactly what Rui planned to do...fight. Holding his daughter in one hand, Rui dialed Owen's number with the other. He needed help if he wanted to win the race for Autumn's heart.

AUTUMN pulled into the parking lot behind No Limit Bar & Grille and cut the engine. She dropped her head to the steering wheel, not sure if running away had been the right decision. She never had any real attachment to a man, a family, or a location. An army of one didn't need a team. So what if she, Rui, and Simone made the perfect trio. Had the best weeks of her life, falling in love with Rui and Simone, been a lie? How could she stay in this town, which had become an integral part of her existence, now that Rui had pushed her aside? Maybe it was time to leave Endurance and keep heading south. There were still ample job opportunities in the San Diego area.

A knock sounded on her window. She looked up to find Tommy standing in the lot, peering into her car.

"You okay?" he yelled. "I saw you and Rui arguing in front of the house."

God, this is when she valued the anonymity of a large city. Everyone in Endurance would know she'd moved out of Rui's place within the hour.

"I'm fine," she called back, not opening the door.

"The big race is tomorrow maybe we could help each other."

Oh god, not now. She didn't want a hero. She wanted to be left alone. When she didn't say anything else, Tommy just stood there, waiting.

Realizing he wouldn't go away, she rolled down the window.

Turning to face him, she pasted on a smile. He was a nice guy. Rui had seemed like a nice guy too, she thought.

"Please, know that I appreciate you checking on me, but I really need to be by myself right now."

He leaned in and Autumn noticed how handsome he was. With his pale skin and ginger curls, he had a boyish quality. But, she'd already given her heart to a brainiac with onyx eyes and straight black mane. Rui. She'd slept with him even after seeing he wasn't over his wife. He said he would get Kirsten out of the house, but Autumn wouldn't let her heart trust his words. Not anymore.

He smiled, his lips lifting into a half-crooked movement. "I can understand that," said he, dipping in a little closer.

Autumn could smell the crisp scent of soap and clean male skin. Nice.

"Thanks, Tommy. I value your friendship."

He chuckled then. He lifted a hand and brushed it against her cheek. "You know," he began, "Rui Conners is a dumb genius if he lets you get away."

She was just about to say thank you when his pressed his lips to hers. Autumn was momentarily paralyzed. His lips felt wrong against hers. She stiffened, and he broke away.

"Nothing?" he asked.

With the back of her hand, she wiped her lips. "Well," she paused. Did all the men in Endurance try to solve a woman's problems with a kiss?

"That bad, huh?"

She didn't want to hurt his feelings, but no way did she want a repeat. Damn you, Rui Conner. Tommy, a perfectly fine specimen of a man who loved to run, was totally a no-go.

"Let's just say, I never want you to do that again."

He winced. "Ouch. Run across my male ego with your rocker bottom tennis shoes, you would."

Now it was Autumn's turn to wince. Had she been too harsh?

"Oh, Tom-"

He held up a hand. "Don't apologize. I was out of line."

Her first thought was to disagree, but she halted the words in her throat. It was time to start being true to what she wanted. She'd tried to please everyone. It was time to please herself.

She sighed. "Thanks for understanding. You're a terrific guy."

"But, not for you."

She shrugged. "I think I'm a goner for someone else."

"Speaking of someone else."

They both turned to see Owen crossing the lot, his long legs moving fast.

"You're needed in the bar. Now."

Eyes wide, Autumn shoved her door open. What could be wrong? Getting the window back in place would have to wait.

"What's wrong?" Had something happened to Ivy or Cai? No. He wouldn't need her help. "Is it Rui? Where's Ivy?"

"Nope and Ivy's out on an errand." Owen barely glanced at Tommy. "Save your moves for tomorrow, bud. I need Autumn inside."

Out of the car, Autumn rushed to catch up with Owen. Who would come for her?

"Rui be reasonable," Kirsten railed. "Where am I going to stay? It's race season."

He cared, but not enough to keep Kirsten in the house another night. "Save your breath. You're leaving. I've arranged for someone to drive you to Sacramento."

When he brought Autumn back home, he wanted no sign of Kirsten within a thirty-mile radius.

"Be reasonable. How about be honest," he charged. "Why do you want back in our lives?"

In the years since their divorce, not once had Kirsten hinted that she wanted to be a part of their family. Rui had prayed, hoped, and wished but nothing changed. Finally, he had a woman who could share in his life. Autumn loved being at home with him and Simone. Though she'd never told him so, she took joy in running their household, in planning special meals for them to share, in teaching Simone how to coordinate her clothes and dance. She loved them more than Kirsten ever did.

"Fine," she huffed. "I've been offered my own talk show here in the US," she beamed. "My agent thinks the family angle would attract a broader audience."

Rui stared at his ex incredulously. Who was she kidding? Kirsten did not have a family-centric bone on her plate, least of all in her body.

"Being a mother and raising a family isn't an angle, Kirsten. Don't you get that?"

She threw up her hands. "Of course I do. That's why I want you and the nanny to take care of Simone. Like I said, I won't come between you two. I'm more than willing to-"

"Stop. Don't say it," he growled. God, why had he never noticed that Kirsten's inhibitions had no limits? No wonder she'd succumbed to temptation within months of leaving him in Endurance.

"Okayyy," she crooned, a teasing smile on her lips. "Just trying to make everyone happy."

He snatched her up. "Did your daughter look happy when she ran to her room in tears? Did Autumn look happy when she packed her bags and left me?" he raised his voice, furious he'd allowed this to happen. "Do I look happy?" he roared, breathing through his nose. "You've managed to wreck our home not once but twice." A small voice whispered that he had a role in allowing Kirsten to hold his life captive. He should have moved on years ago. With Autumn he'd been ready, but now was it too late?

For the first time since her arrival, Rui recognized a real emotion cross his ex-wife's face, confusion. She would never understand him, yet he understood her too well.

"When you leave this time, don't come back without asking me first. I'm going to look in on our daughter."

When he walked away, Kirsten didn't follow. Rui opened Simone's door and froze. The bed was empty.

CHEST heaving, Autumn caught up with Owen. He gripped his elbow.

"What's going on?"

He kept moving through the back door of No Limit. The back of the bar and grille held an addition with a small kitchen, a dining area, and a television room. There were three bedrooms above stairs and one bath.

"Go see for yourself," he said pointing to the door leading into the bar.

Crossing the room, Autumn stood on tip-toes and peered in the square pane in the door.

Simone sat on her bike in the middle of the bar. Autumn turned and stared at Owen. Eyes red, with tears streaming down her face, Simone had parked her Schwinn front and center. Autumn's chest clenched. Where was Rui?

"She's your ward," he frowned. "I tried to calm her down." He ran a large hand through his blond tresses. "It didn't work."

"Were your scowling like you are now?"

He rubbed his chin as if to ponder the question. "Not sure," he said. "My wife's not here. There's a heartbroken little girl and a bike in the middle of my floor."

Owen was a good guy, but he had two speeds, grumpy and grumpier.

"I called Rui too, but I think you might be what she needs."

Autumn had never been someone to be needed. Rui had made her feel desired for a time, but in the end, he wanted more than he was willing to give. Autumn could admit she was tolerant, maybe to a fault, but she didn't share.

"Autumn, are you here?" Simone called.

Owen raised a brow like Simone's outcry had proven his point.

She tipped her head in acknowledgment and exited the room. Time to earn that final paycheck.

Autumn went to Simone and kneeled.

"Hey, baby girl. What are you doing here?"

Visible tear tracks glistened on the little girl's cheeks and Autumn's heart ached. God, she could see all the disappointments and hurts Simone had witnessed in her short life. She was sorry she would add to the tally.

"You have to come back home now," she said, her small voice cracking.

Autumn swept Simone into her arms. "Oh, honey." She inhaled her powdery scent, so innocent. How could she explain to this child who'd lost her mother, even though Kirsten was vey much alive, that she could never return. "I can't."

Simone placed her head on Autumn's shoulder. She held her tighter.

"But, I heard Daddy tell Kirsten to leave," she sniffed. Autumn's breath hitched. Had Rui followed through? "You can come back home. With me and Daddy."

Autumn pulled Simone's arms from around her neck to hold her hands. "You know how much fun I had staying with you and your father, but it's time for me to move on."

"No," she sobbed. As her voice climbed, each sob more despair-laden than the previous, patrons began to stare. "I want you to go with me to the tea at my school."

Autumn didn't know when this little girl who'd tried to steal her car had won her heart, but she had. Her chest ached for the both of them because she wanted to stay. Motherly love came in many forms. She wanted to be a part of Simone's life, see her graduate, help her pick out a prom dress, cry when she went off to college. What she had to say next, would rip her heart out.

"Simone, your mom will take you," she said wiping away her tears. "You know all the steps and you know how long to steep your leaves."

Simone vehemently shook her head in the negative.

"Kirsten doesn't even like tea. I heard her tell one of her business friends on the phone. She doesn't want to take me. You do. Don't you?"

Of course she did. Autumn wanted to be at every graduation, help her prepare for her debutante ball, for her senior prom, her wedding day.

"Yes, honey. But-,"

Simone tugged Autumn forward, but she held her ground. Where was Rui? How dare he force her to hurt Simone like this.

"Then you come home now. With me," she said tugging at Autumn's hand again.

Whispers could be heard throughout the bar. Autumn could imagine how many text messages and video snippets were flowing through the Endurance hotline.

"Ms. Springfield will be there. You like her. I'll have to talk with your father."

She crossed invisible fingers over her chest, asking forgiveness for the lie.

Just then Autumn felt a presence behind her. The hairs on her arm tingled. She knew who'd entered No Limit.

"Her father agrees that you should come home." Autumn's breath hitched at the sound of Rui's voice.

Home. She didn't have a home anymore. Had she ever?

CHAPTER TWELVE

Rui pulled his bag from the car. Autumn had refused to come back home. He had to convince her that his life with Kirsten ended a long time ago. He wished he had realized it sooner. For too long he'd held on to a semblance of love. Autumn was the woman for him and this morning he would prove it. After the phone call to Owen yesterday, Ivy had arrived in the truck to drive Kirsten to the first hotel in Pine Mountain. Endurance was too small for Autumn and his ex to share the same space. Once Kirsten realized Rui had no intention of allowing her to manipulate him and Simone for television ratings, she'd gladly packed her Louis Vuitton luggage to depart.

Spotting the registration table, Rui threw his athletic bag over his shoulder. He searched the assembled runners, looking for Autumn's cinnamon curls.

Owen and Ivy joined the group with Cai in tow.

Owen tilted his head in greeting while Ivy said, "Morning, Rui."

Ivy stared at him, concern in her eyes. Owen just looked at him and shook his head. Yeah, he'd messed everything up.

"Hi, Mr. Rui."

"Hey, Cai. Good to see you buddy. What's new?"

"Do you want to ride my tree swing?"

Rui kept his eyes peeled for Autumn. "Maybe later," he said absently.

"But, my daddy said you need a knot on your head. I can show you how to get one."

"Cai," Owen warned. "No tattling."

"But, daddy. I still got mine–"

Owen gave his son one look, and the boy clammed up. "Another word and you'll have a tanned bottom, Cai."

Ivy gave Rui an apologetic look. "Sorry," she mouthed.

Rather than offended, Rui agreed he might need a few hard knocks if he lost Autumn for good.

He spotted Hank and Luke at the First Aid station, setting up cots and tables. Returning their greeting, he waved.

Feeling eyes on him, Rui turned. Autumn stood, mouth open, staring at him. He strode straight for her, noticing Tommy Roe watching them both.

She spoke first. "What are you doing?"

"I'm joining the race," he stated matter-of-fact like.

Autumn huffed. "Rui, you hate running."

"True, but I love you. Kirsten is gone."

She gave a lackluster nod. Okay, this might be tougher than he anticipated.

"What does that have to do with anything?"

He noticed that she didn't deny his claim. Maybe, he still had a chance.

"You said you needed a man who'll go the distance for you. So, I'm racing."

Autumn grabbed his hand. "You haven't trained. Rui, this is suicide."

He snagged her around the waist. "You're everything I've ever wanted. I'd rather die at your side, than live another day without you."

Rui hoped he didn't kill his fool self. This idea bordered on madness, but what else could he do to prove his love?

"Oh, no you won't," she denied. "I'm not responsible for you. Not anymore."

God, he was hoping she'd warm up to him.

"You love me, Autumn. I know you do."

A woman's voice crackled through a loud speaker. *Runners, check-in and get your numbers. Team members register at the second tent.*

Rui looked over his shoulder. The other runners were stretching and hydrating. Water bottles littered the curbs. There had to be at least five hundred crazy people prepared to run until their toenails popped off. Craziness, but he'd jack up his feet for a life with Autumn.

"You determined to do this?" she asked, glancing at the starters in their orange vests.

He cupped her face in both hands. "I will do anything to prove to you that I will never betray your trust again. I'm in love with you, Autumn Raine. I'm sorry for hurting you."

"If you're crazy enough to run, then let's do this," she said grabbing his hands and pulling them away from her face. "Keep quiet and stay out of my way. I have a race to win."

So did he, the race for Autumn's love.

DEAR GOD, HE'D BE LUCKY if he lived to see the next sunrise. Rui grunted as he pushed his flaccid muscles to pick up the pace. The scenery was breathtaking. The pine forests were denser in this part of the Sierra Nevada foothills. Rui dug deep and pumped his legs harder. In the race of love he refused to come in second place. Even if it killed him, he would win Autumn's heart. About four hours into the race, he thought he had died, but was in the opposite location of heaven. Rui's lungs, heart, and calves felt as if someone had dipped him in kerosene and struck a match inside his body. Everything hurt. Praise be to the angel of mercy, one of the fifteen hundred volunteers at a medical aid station supplied him with water and a protein bar before he lost consciousness.

"Autumn," he panted, as someone took his pulse. "Please tell me," he coughed, struggling to catch his breath, "you love me before my untimely demise."

Without breaking stride, she glanced over her shoulder at his pitiful self. "I told you to stop running an hour ago."

And he had been tempted to listen to his aching body and ignore his rapid beating heart. But first, he needed her to agree to come home.

"Tell, tell me, you're coming home. Simone needs us, the both of us together. We are a family." Her step faltered. He spoke the truth, but did she believe him?

"That a dying wish? This might be delirium talk."

Rui growled. "Come on, sweetheart," he said, reaching for her. Man, his fingers were trembling. "I love you. My daughter loves you. I want you to be my wife. Say you'll marry and come home."

She looked over and smiled. Rui's heart sped up. Would she say yes?

"Autumn?" he prompted when she didn't say anything else.

"I'll tell you at the finish line," she winked, and then sprinted away.

She rounded the first bend along the American River, and then disappeared from sight.

Shoot. He had to go the distance if he wanted her in his life forever.

THE FOLLOWING MORNING, Autumn scanned the crowd as she crossed the finish line, the first finalist having gone the distance with Rui cheering her on from behind. She'd done it! Simone held pennants in both hands, the words, You're A Winner printed in rainbow colors waving proud. Owen had Cai propped on his shoulders. The temperature, well above eighty degrees, had even the early risers pulling their visors low over leathered foreheads. Instead of standing with the men folk behind the yellow tape, she saw Ivy had decided to set up a portable lawn chair in the First Aid tent with Hank and Luke. Kelby Springfield and a bunch of kids from Simone's class cheered as if Autumn had won the first prize scholarship.

Tired and sweaty, she moved through the crowd, avoiding the runners slumped over their knees, abandoned running shoes, and empty water bottles to reach Simone, the little who cheered the loudest for her. Before she could approach, Rui pulled her in for a hug. His solid body cradling her exhausted limbs. Whew, that hurt. Now that the race had ended, her muscles started to cramp, but it was nice to be back in his arms.

"I'm so proud of you, Autumn," he rasped, her head against his chest. She could feel his wide grin against her hair. "You did it."

She had. She'd qualified for the cash prize. She'd set a goal and crossed the finish line. Last night, as she ran, her path lit by a small handheld LED light, she had a revelation. Rui had messed up, but so had she. Kirsten's indecent proposal was just that. No way would Rui have invited another woman in to share in what they had. Instead of allowing the old hurts to hold her hostage, trapping her in a life she didn't want. She should have fought for their love. Just like music, the race had smoothed her fractured heart, cleared away the emotion. Rui loved her. She loved him. If he asked her again to marry him, and God, she hoped he did, her answer would be yes.

She squeezed him tight. "Thank you."

Simone pulled on the hem of her shorts, drawing Autumn's attention. "I knew you could do it."

The smile covering Simone's face warmed her heart more than any medal ever would. This was her family, and she wouldn't leave them. Not now, not ever.

"Congrats, Autumn," Owen said, clapping her on the shoulder. "Dinner's on me next time you and your family drop by the bar."

So, he saw it too. Sighing, she said. "Thanks, Owen."

"Daddy," Cai said pulling at his father's hair. "Now that Autumn's got her prize. Can I have a bun?"

"What bun, buddy?"

"I heard Ivy say she had a little bun in the oven. Can I have it or do I have to share?"

Rui started to laugh, while Simone looked between the adults, a confused look on her face.

"Congratulations, Owen." Rui's chuckle was jovial.

Owen's jaw fell slack, and then the big man's face split in the widest grin. Taking Cai off his shoulders, he tossed his son in the air. Considering Owen's expression, Ivy hadn't told her husband they were expecting.

"Just wait till it's your turn," Owen pointed at Rui before lowering Cai to the ground. "Come on, buddy. Let's go find out what else your mommy has baking."

"Yeah," Cai cheered.

With the race over, the spectators started to scatter. Somehow, her thoughts remained crystal clear.

"Daddy, Autumn, can I go play in the water fountain with my friends?" Simone asked.

"I'll watch her," Kelby offered. "Autumn, you should probably stretch your muscles before they get cold."

"On it," Rui said, lifting her into his arms. "There's a stretcher in the aid station. I can help."

The tent appeared empty when they arrived. A lot of the runners were still on the grass with their team members massaging the knots out of their tight muscles.

Rui sat Autumn on a stretcher before pulling her damp outer shirt off. When she was down to her sports bra, he used a towel to remove the sweat from her face, chest, and abdomen. Using his left hand, he threaded his fingers in her hair.

"What are you doing?" she asked.

"Taking care of my woman," he said, whispering against her ear.

"Yours, huh?"

"As soon as you agree to be my wife. I don't want to rush you, but I love you so much, Autumn. All my life I wanted to belong. Since we met, for the first time in my life, I feel at home when I'm with you."

Gosh, she'd already decided she wanted a life with him and Simone. If she hadn't been convinced with him nearly killing himself on the trail, she was now.

"Rui," she interrupted.

He touched her cheek. "Let me finish, sweetheart."

Reaching out, she grabbed ahold of his hand, intertwining their fingers. "Go ahead."

"Simone and I are a ready-made family and you're so young. I never want you to feel trapped."

Autumn needed him to understand loving him and Simone, being loved by them, was her dream come true.

"Rui, I've always wanted a family of my own," she said raising his hand to lips and kissing it. "I have that with you and Simone. It's what I want."

"We're at the finish line," he whispered. "Say it."

She knew he wanted an answer to the question he asked during the run.

Rui nipped at her lips and she opened for him.

"Not yet," she teased, releasing his hand. He covered her mouth, and she moaned into his. Her hands found his butt. She grabbed a handful and squeezed. His body was perfection. Gosh, he had on too much clothing. He pushed her hand lower, and fire shot through her core.

"What's your answer, Autumn?"

She could barely think with him so close, her emotions rushing to the surface. "Sweetheart, I want you, but you're killing me."

With her tongue she stroked his lower lip.

"My answer is yes, Rui."

"Thank God," someone said from the rear of the tent. "Please let me out of here before you two do anything else."

Autumn yelped and almost fell off the table.

Hank appeared next to them, his face beet red with embarrassment.

"Damn it, Hank," Rui charged. "Why didn't you say something?"

"Hey, don't get mad with me. I'm supposed to be here, Mr. Naughty Professor."

Autumn blushed. She and Rui had gotten carried away.

Hank stormed out of the tent, tossing a, "Congratulations on your engagement. Here's hoping a certain teacher will let me put a spring in her step."

Rui looked at her, and they both started to chuckle. Kelby's focus centered on her kids and rehabbing an old farmhouse she'd purchased a few months back. Hank might have unwittingly signed up for a marathon adventure if he really wanted a chance with the reclusive woman.

"Sorry, I should have known better. We'd better get back to the others. There are a lot of kids here, maybe some of them need a babysitter."

"You never had to worry about winning the race," he whispered. "As the wife of a tenured professor, your tuition is covered."

Autumn wasn't worried. Living with Rui she'd learned to balance school, work, and family. Along the way she'd found love too. She would've discovered a way to reach her goal if the outcome had been different. But, she was thankful her hard work had benefited her physically and emotionally.

Throwing her arms around his neck, she said. "Then, we, husband-to-be, have a tea to attend." Winning the race had been important, but sharing it with Rui and Simone made it special.

AUTUMN SAT AT SIMONE'S table, the Terra Cotta tea set arranged before them. The school's gymnasium had been transformed into a beautiful parlor.

"Are you ready for your first cup of tea?" Simone whispered next to her.

Autumn beamed at the little girl, dressed in a pink lace dress with matching tights and gloves. Even though Kirsten had left California, she'd ordered the dress special for Simone's first mother-daughter tea.

"How many sugars?" Rui asked.

Autumn frowned at him. He insisted on joining them and Simone had jumped for joy. The other mothers had gotten teary-eyed.

"None," Autumn replied.

"How about you try this one on to sweeten the deal?" he said reaching into his pocket.

Autumn saw the black velvet box before he opened the top. A perfectly round pearl nestled in a halo of white diamonds sparkled in the bright lights. Rui lowered himself to one knee, and then grunted in pain. Yep, trying to run a long-distance race without a modicum of training had kicked his butt.

"Autumn Raine, you came into my life and ran away with my heart." Moved by his declaration, she covered her trembling lips with a shaky hand. A single tear slid down her face and Rui brushed it away. "Will you do me the honor of wearing my ring and marrying me as soon as we can plan a wedding?"

Simone and the other children stared in wide-eyed disbelief. Autumn could hardly belief it herself. Rui Conners, the not-so-handy man of her dreams, wanted a family with her.

"Yes," she heard her little girl say, but Autumn kept her eyes on Rui.

"Really? You truly want to get married right away?"

"Yep," he groaned. "Because I'm not doing another race to prove my love if you get cold feet." He laughed.

Autumn reached for the ring, but Rui snagged her hand. "Does this mean I'm off the market?"

"Of course. The moment you gave me a ride, you were mine. My answer is yes," she grinned. "I'm always hot when you're near, professor," she whispered.

"Good. After the wedding, we're all hopping a plane to Florida before going on our familymoon," Rui stated.

Autumn laughed, "What's in Florida?"

Rui swept her up in his arms. "We have another wedding to attend, but I want you to have my band on your finger before I take you around my college buddies."

"Who's getting married?"

"Logan Masters. He's an old friend from my Johns Hopkins days."

"Sounds like fun," Autumn said kissing Rui on the cheek.

Rui stroked his goatee. "Knowing the Masters' family, there's bound to be some drama."

Her aunt had been wrong. Finding love was like a race, not a coin toss. There were intervals of love and loss along the journey. Cultivating an everlasting love required staying the course sometimes and letting go at others. Looking at her new family, Autumn smiled, ecstatic that her days of flying solo were over. The reward, a home in Rui's heart, had been worth going the distance.

Note from Siera London

Thank you for reading GOING THE DISTANCE. There are four novels in this series. Staying The Course, Going The Distance, All Out of Love, and Enduring Christmas. So if you enjoyed Rui and Autumn's story, please do me a solid by leaving an Amazon, Goodreads, and Bookbub review.

Missed some of the Men of Endurance series? Here's the series page link: https://amzn.to/2T24A2u

Also by Siera London
The Men of Endurance Series

- ¥ Staying The Course
- ¥ Going The Distance
- ¥ All Out of Love
- ¥ Enduring Christmas

The Bachelors of Shell Cove Series

- ¥ Chasing Ava
- ¥ Convincing Lina
- ¥ Catching Rebecca
- ¥ Claiming Janna
- ¥ Second Chance Christmas
- ¥ Blindsided: A Lady Guardians Crossover Novella

The Lunchtime Chronicles Series

- ¥ Whipped
- ¥ Thick Cut
- ¥ Prime Ripped

The Fiery Fairy Tales Series

- ¥ Chasing Flames
- ¥ Concealing Fire
- ¥ Commanding Heat

The Kelvinian Warrior Series

- ¥ Cindra: A Paranormal Cinderella Tale

Detective MaKenzie Young Series
¥ The Last File

All Out of Love
A Men of Endurance excerpt
By
Siera London

CHAPTER ONE

Weddings triggered Kelby Springfield's gag reflex. Since she'd slipped into the lacy peach-colored bridesmaid's dress and rhinestone sandals two hours earlier, the urge to hurl had increased tenfold. And not because of the weird potato salad and the blackened yeast rolls the Endurance townsfolk scratched their heads about either. For the big day to feel special, a woman pretended to be a princess, and a man, the savior, her hero. The truth for Kelby, however, was her "prince" had been a lying, cheating, arrogant megalomaniac who made her doubt every decision she made during her three-year stint in matrimonial jail. Just thinking about a man and whispered promises made her spitting mad. She wasn't interested in Mr. Right, Mr. Tight, Mr. Kong, or Mr. Thong. Kelby needed money to pay her little sister's college tuition and a permanent teaching position at the elementary school. That's it. So her fourth-grade teacher colleague, Xenobia Yardell, setting up a blind date with Gordie from that N2U Matchmaking app was a big fat, not-going-to-happen.

Unfortunately for Kelby, Xenobia's date: Peyton, had loaded up his neon green Kia Soul with Gordie; and drove the sixty-four miles from Zolusa Creek to Endurance. What should have been a low-key wedding reception had escalated into a full-scale, high stakes game of hide-and-seek. Thanks to the blistering May heat, the lace clung to her ample chest like expensive plastic wrap, not to mention the plumping sensation happening to her feet. Think popping the champagne cork. Tommy's Park, with its manicured Ponderosa Pines and giant Valley Oaks, plush with green leaves, did little to shield the central California sun. Several of the children had abandoned shoes and socks for a dip in the lake. Women with their faces protected under colorful wide-brimmed sun hats congregated around gingham-draped picnic tables, watching the bride and groom lead Blanco Brown's "The Git Up" © line dance. Taking in the sight, Kelby sighed. "I should have worn a hat."

Xenobia walked up to her, a twinkle of mischief in her hazel eyes. "Smile."

Classic Xenobia lacked preamble or subtlety. She described herself as pretty, round, brown, and too old to clown. Considering the pretentious existence of Kelby's life in Sacramento, she could appreciate her friend's directness. What she couldn't abide: being roped into man drama.

"Why, X?" Kelby demanded using her friend's nickname. The thing about living in a small town was everyone worked to create a sense of community, an extended family, so to speak. A level of trust existed between the citizenry that allowed its members to be vulnerable yet safeguarded by the strength of the unit. Twelve months ago, the town of Endurance had welcomed Kelby with open arms. It was the kind of place where she knew the names of the family pets, when grandparents visited from out of town, and who made the best peach cobbler at the county fair. But Kelby didn't trust easy, so she asked questions. And since her past was her own-she had no intention of divulging her secrets or the reason for her suspicious nature. Xenobia understood that about her.

X smiled, though the expression was pinched. "Because Peyton is watching me," she sang more than spoke the last words. "Give Gordie a chance, Kelby. He might surprise you."

Kelby threw up her hands to avoid shaking her friend. "A surprise is finding out your hair gel is flammable," she exclaimed. "I'm not giving him a chance or a second glance." Why was X pushing this? "He lives in his mother's spare bedroom. I promise," Kelby clapped her hands together to emphasize her point, "this isn't a love match."

Sometimes she wondered what people thought of her. What about her personality said this overgrown mama's boy in his Osh K'osh B'Gosh™ could be her Prince Charming? Not that she was looking. Kelby was all out of love. As soon as this fiasco ended, she needed to have a long conversation with her matchmaking friend.

"But—"

"The answer is no," she said, dropping both hands onto her hips. "He looks like a melted milk dud in a onesie."

Xenobia shrugged, her inky black locks luminescent in the summer light. Along with the same peach lace sundress, she wore a small diamond stud in each ear, a thin gold hoop through her left nostril, and a bold tattoo of a motorcycle covered her center chest. The words: Lady Guardians, formed an arc over the handlebars. Kelby never asked for details on the female biker club. X never offered.

"I thought those were capri pants," she snickered.

Kelby rolled her eyes. "For men?"

She laughed. X laughed till tears gathered at the corners of her eyes.

"Okayy... maybe the clothes are a little tight and the body could use a rebuild, but..." she perked up, "He showed up at a wedding. Girl, you could be his wifey."

"Seriously, I might need a friend upgrade."

Xenobia gasped. Her hand covering her mouth. "That's just mean, Miss *Every Man Is A Friend*," she grinned.

"Whatever. And it's not funny." It kind of was, but Kelby would never admit it. She relished her alone time—especially after years of living under a political microscope. "Who invites two complete strangers to somebody else's wedding?" Exasperation colored the words, most of it authentic. "Get rid of them."

Though Gordie had chatted with her a few times via the N2U Let's Get Social group, actual dates were optional, not an expectation. N2U was like Facebook, for the socially awkward dating crowd. Instead of individual hook-ups, subscribers joined groups to chat with others who shared similar interests.

"But Peyton is so funny," she wiggled her brows. "And he's cute too."

That was an understatement. The man with the unisex name looked runway model perfect. Kelby sighed and wiped the perspiration from her top lip. "X, there's a halo around his ring finger and his eyebrows are waxed."

All of a sudden, her friend's face fell. "So, you're saying he's married, cheating, and metrosexual?"

Looking down at her friend, Kelby nodded. "At the very least."

Xenobia had taken the initiative to register them for a one-month free trial on the dating app, but her motives remained a mystery. They both seemed to be hiding in plain sight. Xenobia had her reasons for leaving the East Coast behind. Nobody found this hidden gem of one thousand, three-hundred-thirty-seven inhabitants by mistake. Everyone had a story of the tumultuous road that led them to Endurance. Distractions came in many forms. For X, it took the shape of completely wrong-for-her men, like Peyton and Gordie. The revelation led Kelby to think her friend had met Mr. Right and he'd screwed it up big time.

A wicked gleam flashed in Xenobia's eyes. "I'll take care of Peyton. You just smile real pretty till I get back."

"Why?" Kelby wondered what her friend had in store for their online Romeos.

"Because Gordie's headed this way with two paper plates full of potatoes," she giggled.

Kelby's head shot up. "What?" she exclaimed.

"I hear wedding bells—wait, those might be dinner bells." A rueful smile spread across Xenobia's face.

Kelby had gotten herself out of one disastrous marriage. No way would she consider another. The move from the city to Endurance had been good for her recovery.

"Where is he?" Kelby demanded, prepared to run in the opposite direction.

Xenobia glanced around her. "There," she pointed in the direction of the lake's edge.

Kelby pivoted on her heel, allowing her eyes to track the movement. Once her eyes hit the final destination she gasped. On Gordie's plate, loomed a tower of smoked meats, potatoes, sliced pies, and a hunk of wedding cake. Dear heaven, did he think he paid for an all-you-can-eat buffet? Quick, she snatched her friend's hand out of the air. "Don't. He might get the idea I'm looking for him."

Too late for that. Gordie had a determined look on his face. Kelby wasn't sure if it had to do with reaching her or the physical exertion. If she started sprinting now, she could reach the parking lot before he crossed half the distance.

"Running won't work girlfriend," X warned, her tone amused. "That weird RoboCop© look he's giving you, says he likes the chase."

She'd taken one step when she remembered a pertinent fact. "Shoot, I rode in the wedding wagon." The walk back to her rented farmhouse wearing Cinderella's slippers would take forty-minutes minimum in this heat. Just great. Resigned to her fate, she steeled her spine, prepared to give Gordie a gentle, but firm, not-in-a-bazillion-years talk. But fate had other plans. A familiar appealing scent reached her first—crisp, woodsy, and warm. Through lowered lashes she spotted a large pair of hand-stitched cowboy boots standing toe-to-toe with her.

Up... -up her eyes climbed surveying the sinewy territory. Hank Stewart with all his tall gorgeousness stood before her. He smiled at her, those perfect white teeth drawing her attention to his full mouth. In his early thirties, his crooked nose and chiseled features had a manly quality she found alarmingly attractive. They were friends, nothing more—not really. A glance here, a longer than necessary conversation when he attended parent-teacher functions, a touch there—yeah, friend stuff. His eyes, deep with whiskey notes met hers, and instantly the blood rushed in her veins. Friends.

Good friends caused a rise in blood pressure. She'd read something about the phenomena on Facebook.

"Hey, Xenobia," he said, not looking away.

The deep timbre of his voice had Kelby's mouth watering and a warning alert sounded in her head. Run away she thought.

Her friend, enjoying Kelby's awestruck silence, laughed. "Hey, big fella. What's up with you?"

"Looking for Kelby." At the sound of her name, she looked up to find his rich brown eyes still directly on her.

"I need your help," he said rubbing a hand over his chin scruff.

Before she could answer, he reached for her hand, enclosing her fingers with his. Instead of leading her away, he waited, holding her.

Interesting," Xenobia muttered. "If you two would excuse me."

"Don't leave," Kelby said, her voice low and sharp.

"You spend time with your friend," she chuckled at the last word.

Xenobia darted away without so much as a, call me. See, this was the reason Kelby hadn't objected to the N2U subscription. Posting, texting was safe. Touching, especially Hank Stewart, rendered her speechless. He stepped forward, his formidable size dwarfing her, his scent consuming her. Hank had been a good friend, a dedicated school volunteer, and a sexy bit of eye candy in her fantasies. Use words, she prompted.

"Sure" she heard herself say. "I'll help if I can." Xenobia-forgotten. Peyton-forgotten. Gordie-

As they cut through the crowd, she couldn't help but notice his powerful build. His thighs looked like they could carry her for days. When his thumb stroked across her knuckles her brain short-circuited. Was he even aware of the caress? A single woman of twenty-eight should not be distracted by a man's touch. But, this was Hank *Just A Friend* Stewart. She spied his backside again. Man, did he do a pair of jeans justice.

"Caught you looking." This came from said man with the tight buns.

Kelby's head shot up to find Hank's rich brown eyes alight with amusement. Not smiling, she gave him a disapproving glare that worked on her third-grade students. "A woman only gets caught if she wants to, Hank Stewart."

"So, I've heard," he chuckled. "Do I get to keep you?"

Kelby's heart rate surged. Why had Xenobia abandoned her? The man was quite possibly the only walking, talking, human smoothie, sweet and satisfying. She should probably change the subject.

"Where's Elliott?" The ten-year-old, with his dark blond hair and caramel brown eyes, looked the mirror image of his father. In a decade, he'd be a heartbreaker.

Hank's eyes crinkled at the corners as if he recognized her tactics.

"Rode in with Chadwick and Sherron. Now, back to you being caught by me."

The town's pediatrician and local cupcake baker were newlyweds. Chadwick had a two-year-old, James, from his previous marriage. Sherron seemed content with the family being just the three of them for the near future. Kelby understood. The decision to enter motherhood should include more than two warm bodies and a marriage contract. Contracts could be broken. She needed to remember smooth-talking men were trouble.

"Ah, Hank...where are you taking me?"

"Some of the wedding guests aren't taking too kindly to the potato salad bar."

Yep, she had overheard a group of the town gossips talking about the bowls full of peeled eggs, boiled Idaho spuds, and yellow mustard.

"You got something to do with the potato salad not being made?" she quizzed. "I mean I've got to put a potato, pickles, eggs, mayonnaise, and mustard on my tissue-thin plate, and then mix all this stuff together."

"Owen left me in charge before driving Ivy over to the hospital in Pine Valley."

The Tates, Ivy and Owen owned the No Limit Bar and Grille, a local meeting place for most folks, except Kelby. Too much information flowed through those walls, so she kept her eyes forward, her mouth shut, and sailed pass the doors when she came into town.

"You were his first choice," she asked, disbelief in her tone. The picture of Hank with an apron and spatula didn't quite gel with his rugged persona. He had a fantastic frame, not too lean, with broad shoulders, and a waist defined enough to know he worked hard and ate well. But she tended to glimpse him with No Limit takeout more than Ma Hildie's grocery bags.

"Boy howdy, woman...you've got a wild tongue."

"And?" she wiggled her arm in his grip. She couldn't free herself. Three years of listening to a man chastise her had created a short fuse easily lit. "Let go," she hissed.

"Hold on a minute." He tugged her in his direction. "I happen to like your mouth," he whispered. "Ivy went into labor before she could whip up the southern-style potato salad and the yeast rolls."

Kelby quieted, but stiffened at the mention of the new baby. Everyone talked about the joy of parenthood, no one warned a woman of how inadequate she could feel when conception never happened. How a man who claimed to love grew to resent a wife's inability to command a body not under her control.

"Kelby?" Hank had stopped walking. "What's wrong?"

Shaking off the melancholy, she pasted on a smile. "Nothing," she stammered. "You need me to help you with the deconstructed potato salad?"

He narrowed his eyes as if he knew she'd changed the subject on purpose. "That'd be nice. But if you have something more pressing—"

"Nope," she interjected. "I'm all about the studs," she blundered. That's it, broadcast the internal dialogue, Juliet to Romeo. "I meant to say, spuds. Potato spuds."

A slow grin spread across Hank's face, lending to an almost boyish quality. "I volunteer for any stud work you might require."

Good gravy, her insides melted faster than a Popsicle left on a picnic table. And, a feeling just as sappy sweet flooded her belly.

With a denial poised on the tip of her tongue, she opened her mouth to dispel any notion she might find him remotely attractive when a winded, but focused Gordie turned in her direction. No. No. No. Why in the Mary-had-a-little-lamb was this happening to her?

"Kiss me," she blurted.

Hank's brow creased. "Can I at least take you to dinner first?"

A fresh wave of perspiration bloomed on her skin and with it, a healthy dose of panic gripped her.

Grabbing him by the lapels, she yanked his face down to hers. "No," she snapped. 'Do it now."

Cutting a glance at Gordie, she noticed he'd slowed his pace, but still advanced. Her stomach knotted. She blanked her mind, angled her head to the side, and pressed her mouth to Hank's. That blankness had been a temporary state. Hank pulled her in close, and slowly coaxed her lips apart. When he slipped inside, she was a goner. The man knew how to stoke a woman's fire.

The kiss quickly became harder, deeper, and God help her, sweeter. Move over hamburger. He tasted better than prime cut beef with a vintage wine. Like a hungry man offered his first solid meal, he devoured her. The stubble covering his chin felt rough against her cheek. She liked the contrast. His gruffness to her silky smooth. Somewhere in between her threading her fingers into his thick mane and his tongue tangling with hers, Kelby heard a few gasps, some cheering, and a chorus of whistles. Hank cupped the back of her head, and she could have sworn they both groaned in unison.

When the kiss ended, she tried to pull back, but a strong arm banded around her waist, anchoring her in place.

"Woman," he breathed, jagged and fast. "If you've been wanting to kiss me like that, you should have told me you loved me a long time ago."

Love. She hesitated. Had she wanted the spark she felt whenever Hank was near to ignite? No. Maybe, but what if she chose the wrong man...again. Would her heart and self-esteem mount a full recovery? She had her priorities, and kissing Hank was nowhere on the list. But, on the other hand, the list was pretty short.

"Kelby?" He waited; his nose pressed into her neck.

Her stomach flipped. Why did he need an answer? In the eighteen months since her divorce, she'd managed to avoid anyone with muscles and a mustache. But Hank with his watchful eyes, easy smile, and generous nature had been impossible to ignore. As she'd gotten to know the town, she'd learned Hank was the kind of man she could fall for...if she was looking. Which, she wasn't.

"Well... I'm kind of all out of love," she whispered. Maybe. Hank's kiss stirred a hunger her body had suppressed even before Bradford had demanded a divorce.

He chuckled, the sound rich and melodic compared to the noisy jumble surrounding them.

"You sound unsure, darling."

Only when his lips touched hers, Kelby decided. "I plead the Fifth," she said.

"Hmm," Hank said, "I'll take my chances all out of love too."

Kelby let herself enjoy the rush of surprise. The words held a different meaning coming from his insanely kissable lips. That arm around her waist, pulled her up closer to his chest, and she felt more than witnessed his pleasure at touching her. Before she realized what was happening, Hank captured her chin.

"I get to choose what happens next," he growled, before covering her mouth with his.

Keep reading All Out of Love: https://amzn.to/39H5EiE

CONNECT WITH SIERA

Siera London is the USA Today Bestselling & Award-winning author of contemporary and paranormal romance, romantic suspense, and crime fiction. She crafts stories of diverse characters navigating the challenges and triumphs to find lasting love. Intelligence, wit, emotion, drama, and romance are between the covers of every Siera London novel. Siera lives in Virginia with her husband, and a color patch tabby named Frie.

If you want to see my travels, and my grandbabies, as well as my book updates, sign up for my newsletter: https://landing.mailerlite.com/webforms/landing/i2s4f9

And, I'm on social media, too.

Facebook Author Page: https://www.facebook.com/authorsieralondon

Amazon Author page: http://amzn.to/1Oce1Ht

Goodreads: https://www.goodreads.com/siera_london

Bookbub: https://www.bookbub.com/authors/siera-london

Twitter: https://www.twitter.com/siera_london

Instagram: https://www.instagram.com/sieralondon

Pinterest: https://www.pinterest.com/sieralondon

https://www.sieralondonauthor.com

www.ingramcontent.com/pod-product-compliance
Lightning Source LLC
Chambersburg PA
CBHW020446270626
47155CB00022B/1682